FEMI

B. LOVE

#BTHEBEAST

Copyright © 2020 by B. Love

All rights reserved.

No part of this book may be reproduced in any form or by any electronic or mechanical means, including information storage and retrieval systems, without written permission from the author, except for the use of brief quotations in a book review.

❦ Created with Vellum

INTRODUCTION

Big Sigh.

This book has been a long time coming. Two or three years, I believe. A part of the reason why it took so long was because I didn't want readers to compare Femi and her partner to Rule and Camryn.

For your own sake, do not go into this story expecting Femi to be anything like Camryn or Asylum to be like Rule. It is simply not fair to them.

I guarded this book with my life. I didn't want to share it with the world. That's mainly why I didn't want to publish it on Amazon. Their story is sacred to me. It's the first book I've done that had more drama than romance. It's not packed with sex. In fact, there are only three sex scenes, and two of them are implied. They only go on one real date, and that's in their home.

But there is love here. And passion. And sensuality.

I don't really know how to categorize this book. And I think that's another reason why it was so special to me. For the first time in years, I was able to write without having to worry about genres, charts, rankings, reviews, or what anyone would think about it. Without having to worry about presenting something that is "Typical B. Love." I've done such a good job branding myself that if I do anything different these days, it's met with criticism.

Alas, I'm five years and over 100 books in and Sis needs to switch shit up Offering this story as a drama in paperback form was one way for me to do so. So thank you, for your support.

This book was for me, Femi, and Asylum... but I'm so very honored to share it with you. Get ready for a wild ride, and I hope you enjoy their story as much as I did! If you did, please send me a review via email at emailblove@gmail.com.

1

Femi

She kept her head down low, not wanting to risk anyone seeing her. Though Femi feared no man in her life, she was smart, and she knew the consequence for what she'd done would be murder if she was caught. It wasn't every day that she disobeyed a direct order from The Bosses in Peru, but this... this was worth it.

Well, she thought it was worth it. Now that she'd had

to uproot her entire life and leave the drug dynasty that she'd created... Femi couldn't say for sure.

Q told her that he'd meet her by Gate 13. Once she passed it, she stopped and slowly tilted her head in its direction. Though her eyes immediately landed on a man wearing what Q said he'd have on, she didn't walk over to him right away. It could have been a trap or a stranger who would draw attention to her if she approached him for no reason. The Bosses had eyes everywhere, not just in Peru. If Femi was going to survive, she would have to be smart and strategic.

If she had her phone, she would have called him, but she left it in Peru. That's why she was meeting him. Q had, essentially, her new life in his hands. Cupping her hands together, she twiddled her thumbs around one another and checked her surroundings before slowly walking over to him. Femi stood by his side, giving him time to look up from his phone and notice her. If he recognized her, that would be her sign that he was the tall, black man who was supposed to be waiting for her dressed in all black. If not, she would wait until he arrived.

Clearing her throat, she looked to the left, causing him to lift his eyes. A smile slowly crept across his face as he turned in her direction.

"Feel like I'm standing next to a motherfuckin' living legend. Follow me outside, Denaé."

Denaé. That was the fake name he'd given her for identification purposes. It would take nothing for The Bosses to use their federal connections to search for cars and apartments recently acquired by women named Femi. So as much as she loved her name and the meaning behind it, Femi knew that she'd have to temporarily give it up to secure her safety while in Memphis, TN. Slowly, Femi followed behind Q, keeping her head low at all times.

Her features were distinct. All it took was one look into her eyes and she'd be made out. Absently pushing her dark sunglasses further up her nose, Femi released a heavy sigh. Never one to take on the battles of others, she couldn't believe the blood that had spilled on her hands. For someone she'd known for less than six months at that! Camryn Meadows had come to Peru temporarily and shook a lot of shit up. And now, she was back home, living in peace with her family while Femi was struggling with accepting the fact that she no longer had one.

It was hard enough not having her family of origin. Her bloodline. The drug cartel she ran had become her everything. And in the blink of an eye, the release of one bullet, that was now gone, too.

Once they made it outside, Q began to talk. He didn't bother to stop walking as he led her across the airport parking lot.

"Your new name is Denaé Freeman. If you want to still use Femi, you can, just make sure every legal document you use has your new name on it so they can't trace you. Your ID has you with dark brown eyes and brown locs, so if they do a facial recognition search it won't be an immediate match. Depending on how deep and long they run it, they can still find you, so you need to make sure you lay low and do nothing to draw attention to yourself."

He led her to a white, 2018 Mercedes Benz. Femi accepted the keys he offered her. "This bag has your new ID, birth certificate, and social security card. The keys to your apartment are in here as well. The apartment complex thinks you're a transcriptor who works from home, so they aren't expecting much traffic in and out of your place. Anything suspicious will alert the guards. Do you need anything else from me?"

Nothing he could give.

He couldn't go back in time and keep her from putting a bullet between Mateo's eyes.

With a shake of her head, Femi accepted the black bag he handed her.

"Keep calls under sixty seconds when you're speaking to someone The Bosses know you associate with. Try not to call repeatedly, either. I would recommend having them get a second line that they use to talk to you on for longer conversations."

"Thanks," she mumbled, almost in shock of her own voice. Femi hadn't spoken to anyone in three days. Was it possible to forget what your own voice sounded like?

"You got my number if you need anything else."

With a nod, Femi pulled his payment out of her purse and handed it to him. Getting inside the car, she held her breath until she could no longer see him in the rearview mirror. As she released it, she pulled the phone out of the bag and went through the process of setting it up. When she was done, her first call was to Camryn. After telling her that she'd meet up with her once she was settled into her apartment, Femi disconnected the call and drove away.

2

Femi

Sitting in the back of the café by the emergency exit, Femi watched every person that came in and went out. She'd purposely arrived thirty minutes early to scope out the scene. While she knew Rule and Camryn were worthy of her trust, nothing would ever make her totally rely on the protection of another human being. Especially right now.

She watched as Rule held the door open for Camryn, and a grin threatened to tug up the corners of her lips – Femi wouldn't let it form, though. When Rule's eyes landed on her, he took Camryn's hand and led her over to Femi's table. Standing, she extended her hand to shake theirs, but Camryn pulled her in for a tight, warm hug. It took Femi a second to return it, seeing as though she hadn't been hugged in over a decade, but when she did... it felt right.

"I'm so glad you made it in safely," Camryn confessed, taking the seat next to Femi as Rule sat across from both of them. "Tell us what happened, Femi." Camryn's hand covered Femi's on top of the table, and she had to keep herself from pulling it out. The only woman that had ever shown Femi affection was... well... there hadn't *been* one. Not after her mother.

Femi's lips parted and she released a shaky breath as she casually pulled her hand from underneath Camryn's. Camryn seemed cool, for the most part, but Femi hadn't quite yet figured the whole friend thing out. Right now, she had even less of a desire to. Though her current situation may have called for more support than she was usually willing to receive.

Femi knew who Camryn was before she met her a few months ago. She knew that Camryn was Anthony's stepdaughter. Anthony had become like a Godfather to Femi over the years. Before she met him, she admired that he was one of the few people in the drug game who were able to survive as one of America's Most Wanted. When Anthony moved to Peru, he enlisted the help of Femi and her partner, Tatum, to continue to make money in the streets.

As she grew close to Anthony, he told her about the life he had to leave behind – including Camryn and her mother. When Anthony was murdered, Camryn came to Peru to find answers. They eventually found out who was responsible for Anthony's death, and Camryn wanted revenge. She was graced with a meeting with The Bosses, five elders who controlled the drug world and streets of Peru, but they did not grant Camryn permission to avenge Anthony's death.

The evidence that they found proved that Anthony was working with the FBI, preparing to give them information on Mateo in exchange for his freedom. Because that would have technically classified Anthony as an informant, The Bosses washed their hands with Anthony. Camryn wanted to take matters into her own hands, but Rule wouldn't allow her to. Now, with the danger Femi was in, she hoped Camryn realized how blessed she was to have a husband who kept her from making the decision Femi made.

She knew how hurt Camryn was when she left Peru, and she also felt a bit of obligation to Anthony, so she took matters into her own hands and killed Mateo herself. Now, she was on the run, doing whatever it took to make sure The Bosses didn't take her back to Peru for her punishment.

"I couldn't let what Mateo did slide." Femi's top lip curled as she looked out of the window. "He came to a meeting with The Bosses, basically bragging about what he'd done to Anthony. Later that night, I followed him to a club and put a bullet between his eyes while he was getting head from a stripper."

Femi shrugged as she pulled her glass of water closer.

"Were there any witnesses besides the stripper?" Rule checked.

"I'm on the cameras in the club, but no one saw me go in or out of the room. They assume it was me because I was the only known enemy in the same place as him."

"So... if we could find someone else to take the blame, you'd be safe?" Camryn suggested, to which Femi smiled and shook her head.

"It's not that simple, Camryn." Her smile fell. "Besides, I don't let anyone take credit for my work."

Rule sat up in his seat with a shake of his head. "So what's your next move, Femi?"

She scratched her ear as she looked from him to Camryn. "To rebuild. Here." Rule's head shook, but she continued. "I came to Memphis because I've done my research, and there's only one person capable of going to war with The Bosses if necessary. Asylum."

Rule's eyes snapped shut as he sat back in his seat. Grumbling under his breath, she could barely make out what he said. All she heard definitely was that she was going to drive him crazy just like Camryn. With a smile, Femi continued.

"I want to partner with Asylum and offer him something he can't refuse. My connections as a supplier..."

"Don't mean shit anymore," Rule gritted. "You have no weight or rank as long as The Bosses are looking for you. Who you think gon' willingly go to war with their old, powerful asses just for you?"

"Rule..." Camryn started, but there was no need.

"Someone who knows who the fuck I am and what I have to offer. Asylum can be that one. My partner. And even if he doesn't immediately see it like that, you can help me."

"Hell nah," Rule rejected, standing and lifting Camryn from her seat by her arm.

"We owe her this, Rule. She avenged my father's murder for me after you told me to stand down."

"Stepfather," Rule corrected. "And you're not going to guilt me into this because of that. We ain't in the streets no more, and your ass had no damn business going to Peru, trying to start a war over Anthony, especially after he told you not to from the grave!"

With a huff, Camryn remained silent for a few seconds. "She's the reason I didn't have to take that chance. We owe her. Please, Rule."

Rule sighed in defeat before lowering his hat further onto his head. "Meet with Asylum first on your own. If he doesn't take your bait... I'll talk to 'em."

Camryn squealed and hugged him from the side, and as much as Rule wanted to be irritated by it, his frown was replaced with a smile.

"Thank you so much, Femi, and I promise, I will forever be indebted to you for this. Whatever you need, you got, okay?"

Femi nodded, though she wasn't the type to consistently call in favors. All she needed was Asylum's covering in the streets. If her name was attached to his, she'd be straight. Other than that, Femi would always rely only on herself.

3

Asylum

Asylum's jaw clenched. Anger filled him all over again when he noticed the specks of blood staining his Chanel x Pharrell x Adidas. With a growl, Asylum lifted his foot, prepared to smash the man's brain further in, but he was pulled back by his best friend.

"He learned his lesson," Bailey assured him.

"Fuck we 'bout to body this nigga for anyway?" his other best friend, Diego, asked.

Sucking his teeth, Asylum removed himself from Bailey's grip. "To teach these niggas a lesson."

He scanned the room, looking into every pair of eyes that looked on at him.

"He damn near lost his life because he lost my product." Asylum smiled as he looked down at him. "I take that back – he damn near lost his life because he said, 'You got money, what's one shipment?'" Refusing to get worked up again, Asylum lifted his shirt and used it to wipe his face as he inhaled a deep breath. "Protect my product as if your life depends on it...because it does."

His workers nodded, but they all remained silent.

"Get his bitch ass outta here," Asylum ordered as he walked away.

He went into the multi-stall bathroom in his warehouse and cleaned up before calling Miranda to make sure she was ready for him to come through. There was still a bit of pent-up frustration within him that could only be released through his cum. And if he was going to meet with the infamous Femi, Asylum was going to have to do everything he could to get his mind right.

Before she reached out to him, Asylum was well aware of who she was. He also knew that she was on the run from The Bosses. While he had an idea of what she wanted with him, Asylum still wanted to go into their meeting with an open mind. Because, if half of what he'd heard about Femi was true, she wasn't the type to go to anyone for help. So what could she have possibly wanted with him?

Trying his hardest not to let his curiosity get the best of him, Asylum increased the volume on his radio and let the windows on his 1967 Chevy Impala down. His head bobbed to Sir Charles Jones as he sang about being on his own again. One song seamlessly shifted into another, and by the time Asylum pulled up to Miranda's job, he'd had a mini-concert.

Pulling his phone out of his pocket, Asylum dialed Miranda's number and hoped she answered. He'd prefer if she came outside to get this dick instead of forcing him to have to go in and find her.

"Hey," Miranda answered before chuckling at whatever was being said in her background. "No, ma'am, I'm taking my break in about an hour."

"Nah," Asylum spoke up. "Take that hoe now. I'm outside."

He imagined Miranda grinning in her silence. "I am not going to have sex with you outside, Asylum. And you know you're going to be mad if my wet pussy gets any cum on your seat."

That was true.

"Well meet me somewhere in there since it sounds like your class is full."

Miranda sighed. She worked at a daycare in the heart of the hood, run by the mother of one of Asylum's old business partners – Ransom Castillo.

"My boss is doing walkthroughs right now. I can't leave, bae."

Asylum massaged his temple. He could have called another woman, but Miranda had been his main go-to for the past eight months. They weren't in a committed relationship, but she was the woman he kicked it with most consistently.

"Aight," Asylum grumbled, prepared to disconnect the call.

"Don't call no other bitch, either. I get off at four. You can wait until then."

With a slight roll of his eyes, Asylum disconnected the call. Yea, he had the discipline to wait... he just didn't want to.

4

Asylum

The moment his eyes landed on her, Asylum's dick began to harden. He told himself it was the stored up cum that needed to be released, but that was only half the truth. Femi was bad as fuck, and she walked like she knew it, too.

Her head was lifted high, jet black hair sitting on the

top of her head in a messy bun. Eyes covered with shades, she kept a stone facial expression that matched the black lipstick she wore. The black jumpsuit she wore accentuated her slim frame and wide hips, and Asylum couldn't help but wonder how her stilettos would feel digging into his sides as he dug into her.

Fuck was he saying?

He didn't have missionary sex.

There was no kissing and looking into a woman's eyes.

Running his hand down his neck slowly, Asylum sat up in his seat. There was nothing gentlemanly about him, but he couldn't help but stand in her presence. He needed to see those eyes... because he was sure she was taking him in just as he was doing to her. As if she read his mind, Femi slowly removed her sunglasses. Asylum had to grit his teeth to keep from smiling at the sight of her green eyes peering into his. They were just as piercing as legend said they were.

The streets said when she got angry, they turned dark brown – damn near black. That's how niggas knew they were about to be fucked up. When those eyes changed colors... there was no turning back.

"Thank you for meeting me," was her greeting. She was soft-spoken. Her voice was honeyed. Made sense... quiet power, soothing tone... definitely not worthy of his trust.

"I was curious about what you could possibly want with me. That's the only reason we're having this meeting," Asylum made clear.

She smiled. Licking her lips, Femi tilted her head before tugging the bottom one between her teeth.

"Are you going to invite me to sit down?" Their eyes remained locked for a few seconds before Asylum closed the space between them. Looking down at her, he grabbed the back of the chair closest to her and pulled it back. She kept his gaze as she sat down, paralyzing his breathing. He didn't release it until she looked away. "I take it that means you've heard about my current plight?"

With a chuckle, he went back to his side of the table. When she reached out to him, Asylum offered to meet with her at the hole in the wall fish place he handled most of his business at. The food was good as hell and it maintained a low profile because it was deep off in the hood and away from prying eyes.

"I wouldn't call going against The Bosses in one of the world's biggest drug capitals a plight, Femi."

Smiling with the left side of her mouth, she sat up in her seat. Her voice was just above a whisper when she asked, "Then what would you call it, Asylum?"

Not answering right away, Asylum was forced to sit up as well. She spoke so low, she demanded his attention. He couldn't focus on anything else but the words coming out of her mouth. Maybe she did that on purpose. Maybe that was her way of commanding attention and respect.

"You fucked up, and I assume you expect me to help you fix it."

Her exhale came out heavy as she shook her head. The waitress that had taken his order returned to their table to get Femi's.

"I don't think I'll be here long enough to eat," Femi declined, eyes never leaving his. She waited until the waitress left to say, "I didn't fuck up. Mateo needed to be handled, so I handled it."

"The streets say they told you not to, though."

"They told Camryn not to, not me."

As much as he didn't want to entertain her making

light of the situation, he couldn't keep himself from smiling.

"I like that mouth," he confessed, eyes lowering to her lips as he licked his. "I bet it gets you in a lot of fuckin' trouble."

"Trust me... you have no idea."

Asylum lifted his eyes back to hers. "I'm not going against them."

"I'm not asking you to."

"Then what are you asking?"

"To..." She paused, twisting her mouth to the side. Briefly, her eyes shifted from his. The confidence she walked in with was slowly fading away. "To be for me what your name means."

Protection.

Shelter.

Haven.

Sanctuary.

Even more specifically... refuge for criminals at risk in their home countries.

Asylum sat back in his seat and rolled his neck. Allowed his eyes to focus on the ceiling as she continued to speak.

"I don't need... physical protection. Not like bodyguards and all that bullshit. I walk alone. But... I need you to make it clear in the streets that you fuck with me. That if anything happens to me, they'll have to deal with you. I don't expect you to actually go to war with The Bosses unless they came to your city and tried you. I just need them to believe the threat. They have pretty much blackballed me, so no one is brave enough to even answer my calls right now. If you need a reason, I can offer you my services as a supplier and connect. There's a couple of people in Bogotá and Miami that still fuck with me."

"You come to my city, without my permission, and put a target on our backs. Now you want to use my reputation for your safety, and you expect me to put my team in harm's way if... no... *when* they come for you?"

"I'm telling you, they are not going to come here. At worst, they will send one man for me. Tradition states it should be someone close to me. Tatum. He's lethal, but he's nothing without me. You have nothing to worry about."

"Then why are you here?"

Truthfully, Asylum just wanted to hear her say it. That she needed him. In more ways than one. Because although she sat across from him on some street shit, he couldn't help but want to be for her what her own name meant, too. As he researched her in preparation for their meeting, he looked up the meaning of her name. It was almost a plea. Femi meant love me. And even though there hadn't been any love in his heart for years... there was something about her...

"What do you desire?" Eyebrows wrinkled, Femi opened and closed her mouth. Her head shook in confusion. "Who are you?"

"What does that have to do anything?"

"Are you deflecting because you don't know the answers, Femi?"

"I'm deflecting because that has nothing to do with..."

"I can't be associated with you. You need to leave."

Her head shook as she stood. The chuckle she released was short and low. "They said you were a man of honor and character. Obviously, they described you wrong."

"My honor and character are what will keep me from contacting Tatum and telling him where you are. But that's as far as this shit goes. And if The Bosses do come to Memphis looking for you, I will deliver them to you myself before I let you start a war in my city."

"*I* built this shit," she roared, slamming her closed fist down on the table. Her eyes immediately began to turn brown, and Asylum had to bite down on his bottom lip to stifle a moan. All eyes were on them, but he felt no fear. Not because Femi wasn't to be taken seriously, but because she knew it would be stupid as hell to try anything with him. "If Tatum and I wouldn't have left Memphis, you wouldn't have had a place here. Humble yourself before I make myself your competition and show you why you *never* should have fucked with me."

Femi

She'd been having nightmares for the past three nights. Femi hadn't left her apartment once since her meeting with Asylum. For some reason, she thought he'd help her; now she had to come up with a different solution to her problem. Every night, she envisioned her murder – in the hands of Tatum. The only way he could find her at this point, was if someone set her up and led him to her. That reasoning had her feeling uneasy about trying to link up with anyone else.

There was something about Asylum that she felt she could trust. Up until their meeting, she'd been at peace with the thought of working with him. It wasn't until she began to consider other options that the nightmares started.

When Camryn called her to check on her this morning, she started to not talk to her, but she answered to see if she could convince Rule to meet with Asylum any time soon. Asylum's reputation had preceded him. If anyone could help her rebuild her drug dynasty without having to worry about The Bosses coming after her... it was him. And while her pride made it hard for her to even think about begging for his help, she was definitely open to having a second conversation.

As Asylum stared at her with a hard expression, Femi was wondering if that was a good idea.

Quite frankly, Asylum looked mean as fuck. His eyes were dark, almost lifeless. Very rarely did he smile, but when he did... his eyes did, too. His square head and strong jaw gave him an even more masculine look. Blunt-brown and pink, juicy lips were framed by a nappy, scruffy beard. His hair came down to his ears at the top, braided in small plaits. Tattoos covered his arms and hands... and maybe other places, too. Places his clothing hid. There were two on his face, over his left eyebrow and next to his right eye.

He was fine in a street nigga kind of way... and if Femi was the average woman... she would have been trying to make their relationship personal, too.

Asylum released a loaded sigh and scratched his scalp. His eyes finally trailed over to Rule.

"Don't tell me you've come to me on her behalf, big brother."

Rule smiled. "You know how it go. Happy wife, happy life. The wife wants you to help her, so I want you to help her, too."

"Nah," he muttered, shaking his head as he cupped his hands on top of his desk. "I got enough problems of my own. I don't need hers, too."

"Are you going to talk about me as if I'm not here? The least your rude ass could do is acknowledge my presence."

Not even bothering to look at her, Asylum continued. "It's one thing for her to be on some rah-rah shit with a li'l nigga from the hood. Even if it was a local enemy, I might consider it. But she asking me to put my name and life on the line against The Bosses. They got a whole slew of crazy motherfuckers that'll come for war behind them."

"I told you they won't do that. Mateo wasn't valuable enough for them to go through all of that. If they do anything, they will send Tatum after me. He will try to take me back there for my punishment. That's it."

"If that's it, what you need me for?"

Rolling her eyes, Femi gripped the edge of her seat to keep from getting up and in his face. She hated having to explain shit, repeat herself, or ask for help. So even having to come to him had her emotions spiraling.

"I told you," she gritted, nostrils flaring. "If you spread the word that I'm with you, no one will help Tatum. He won't be able to find me on his own. And even if he does find me, he won't cross you. All I need is your name and for you to spread the word. That's it."

Their eyes remained locked for a few seconds. Femi had made it a habit to learn how to hold off blinking for moments like this. She knew men would often assume she was weak because she was a woman, so anything she could do to prove she had enough masculine energy to match theirs... she did. But with Asylum? It wasn't a matter of blinking first... it was a matter of getting lost in his eyes.

Looking away, she asked Rule to, "Do something."

Rule licked his lips as he looked from her to Asylum. "What if I take on the responsibility of Femi?"

She was about to check him but decided it was probably in her best interest to remain silent.

"What do you mean?"

"She did this for my wife and her stepfather. It's because of her loyalty to Anthony that my wife is back home safely. Without Femi, they would be coming for her. So I do, in fact, owe her." Rule paused and looked at Femi briefly. "If The Bosses want to go to war, I'll battle at your side."

"No," Femi rejected quickly, grabbing his wrist. "I refuse to let you get back in the streets for me."

"It's not up to you. My wife wants you protected, so for her, I'm going to do whatever the fuck I gotta do."

For a brief moment, Femi couldn't help but wonder how that felt. To have someone with unwavering loyalty, devotion, and love at your side. She used to think Tatum was her person. That she could trust him to give her those things. But he made it clear years ago that that wasn't the case. Love had never been a need for Femi, so she hadn't often considered herself lacking... but it was moments like this... when she saw love in human form... that she wondered, what if.

The creaking of Asylum's seat as he sat back pulled Femi's attention back to him. His head nodded slowly as he stared at her.

"Rule is a legend. Not just in Memphis, but in the drug game as a whole. If he and his wife are willing to risk their legit lifestyle for you..." Asylum scratched above his forehead and shook his head – as if he was battling with what he was about to say. Sitting up, he snatched a pen from the cup on the edge of his desk and scribbled something on a sticky note. Standing, he handed the note to her. "Meet me at this warehouse at midnight."

Her eyes sealed as she inhaled a deep breath. That wasn't a definite yes, but it was better than a no. Nodding, she stood.

"Than—"

"Don't thank me, 'cause I ain't doing this for you. Thank Rule."

"Look, if you're going to be an asshole about the shit..."

"Femi," Rule called, standing and gently grabbing her wrist. "Let's go before you fuck up the progress we made."

Grumbling under her breath, Femi fought to keep from letting Asylum know how she really felt as Rule all but tugged her outside. If Asylum thought she was going to deal with his slick-ass mouth on a regular basis, he had another thing coming. Femi tolerated disrespect from no one. She'd die before she let any man get away with it... Asylum included.

6

Asylum

There was no denying it – the more she stayed in his presence, the more she couldn't stand him. If he was the average nigga, Asylum was sure Femi would have tried to kill him by now. That thought alone tickled him. They met at one of his warehouses at midnight, and as the sun began to set, Asylum finally felt comfortable enough agreeing to help her.

He'd asked her a series of questions to see where her mind was at before testing her shooting and fighting abilities. When she grew tired of target practice and beating up the men he'd lined up in front of her, the questions would start all over again. Asylum expected her to give up around four in the morning when she started to throw up. It was clearly a sign of exhaustion, weakness physically... but it seemed to only motivate her to go harder.

She had this thing about independence, and honestly, Asylum was hoping their night together would break her. If anything, it only seemed to make her stronger. On the bright side, he felt more comfortable with not physically being with her twenty-four-seven to make sure she stayed safe. Femi could handle her own against his toughest men. If Tatum did come for her, he would have his hands full.

"That's enough," Asylum called, gaining Femi's attention. Slowly, she lowered the AK47 that she was using and looked over at him. Her chest heaved as she took in deep breaths. "I'll do it."

She handed the gun to Bailey, then went to the corner where her phone, sunglasses, and keys were laying. Figuring she'd try to leave without saying anything to him, Asylum headed to the door. Sure enough, she opened the door without so much as a look in his direction. His hand wrapped around her wrist, stopping her.

With a quiet chuckle, she shook her head and pulled in a deep breath.

"Somethin' on your mind, Femi?"

Cutting her eyes at him, Femi jerked her wrist out of his grasp. "I don't like you. At all."

Asylum laughed. "Good. You going straight home?"

"Nah. I'll probably stop and get some breakfast since it's a new day."

"Cool. I'll put Malcolm on you. He's one of my personal muscles. Any time I have issues, he's the first person I call."

"I told you I don't need bodyguards. I can hold my own."

"If you did, you wouldn't need me."

"I already told you what I need you for..."

"Femi!" he roared, a lot louder than he intended to. "I'm sick of going back and forth with yo' stubborn ass about this shit. If you want my help, you getting all of it. Take your ass on and don't give Malcolm no attitude about it, either."

Her eyes tightened. Jaw clenched. Chest stopped moving. Had her heart stopped beating?

"Who you think you talking to?" she asked, voice low and cold as her eyes turned brown.

Asylum looked over her head before returning his eyes to her. "You the only Femi in here, ain't you? I'm talking to you."

Without blinking, her hand wrapped around his neck, pushing him into the wall. Asylum lifted his hand, keeping his men back as they drew their guns.

"I'm about sick of you," she gritted. "Now I'm trying to be a lady about this shit and submit because I need your help, but keep trying me, Asylum, and I'll have to leave Memphis, too, for putting one between *your* eyes. Am I making myself clear?"

He wasn't sure if it was the way she looked up at him, the calmness of her voice, or her tiny hand trying to wrap around his neck that had his dick growing... but something was turning him the hell on. When she felt it pressing against her, Femi dropped her hand and put some space between them. With a smirk, Asylum pushed himself off the wall.

"What you falling back for now? Huh?" Lowering his head, he invaded her personal space. Wrapping his hand around her neck, he pulled her back into his chest. The sight of her biting down on her bottom lip had him licking his as she scratched at his wrist. "The next time you put your hands on me, it better be to kill me, because I might not be able to keep them boys off ya. I'm not Tatum, and you will respect me..."

"Only if you respect me, too," she countered quickly.

Releasing her neck, Asylum ran his hand down his slowly. "Malcolm will trail you until I make our partnership known. When I'm sure no one will come after you, I will pull him. Is that fair enough?"

Femi rolled her tongue over her cheek before nodding in agreement. "That's fair."

"Cool. Be smart. Stay safe... stay dangerous."

If he wasn't mistaken, Asylum would have sworn he saw her eyes begin to lighten as she fought a smile. Before he could check for sure, she was putting her sunglasses back on as she mumbled, "Yea, you too."

7

Femi

Femi's mood was fucked up because she'd been having the same dream over and over again. Every time she had it, more elements were shown. At first, she only saw herself getting shot. Now, she was able to see her surroundings as well. Femi assumed the dreams would stop when Asylum agreed to help her, but that hadn't been the case. Still, fear was a foreign feeling to her. All she could do was thank God, because, in a sense, the dream was a warning.

When she found herself in the room that she kept seeing in her dream, she'd know what time it was. Now she found herself praying she'd see the person behind the bullet in her dream before they snuck up on her in her reality. While she was aware of The Bosses using Tatum to bring her back if it was necessary, she could only hope he'd be too loyal to be the trigger man. If death was going to come... it would be easier if it came from someone that she hadn't known since she was nine years old.

Before her father died, Tatum was like a brother to Femi. But after he died when she was fifteen, Tatum deemed it necessary to become like a father figure to her. Instead of being her confidant, he tried to rule over her as he continued to teach her the game. Eventually, she began to love him less while her respect for his hustle and street knowledge grew. Before she left Peru, they'd stopped dealing with each other on a personal level altogether. Only discussing business, Femi felt herself losing yet another important person in her life.

Their detachment made it a bit easier to accept, though.

Maybe Tatum pulling the trigger would have been for the best.

He wouldn't allow her to suffer.

Though Femi had no appetite, she knew she'd need to put something on her stomach. Deciding to make herself a smoothie, she headed for the kitchen, stopping in her tracks at the sound of the doorbell ringing. The only person who knew where she lived was Q, and she no longer had a use for him. So who was at her door?

Femi grabbed the pistol she kept in the hallway under her end table and quietly walked to the door. She always kept a towel at the bottom of the door and a piece of paper towel in the peephole to ensure that no one would know she was home unless she absolutely wanted them to. As carefully as she could, Femi pulled the towel out of the peephole and looked out of it. With a roll of her eyes, she sighed at the sight of Asylum.

The weight of her body pressed against the door.

"What?"

"Open the door, Femi."

"Why? And how do you know where I live?"

Asylum chuckled. "Just open the door. It's hot as hell out here."

She didn't want to, but Femi smiled. She also didn't want to be happy to see him, but a part of her was. He had a smart-ass mouth, but she liked looking at his sexy, mean ass. And he was probably the only man in quite some time who could possibly handle her. Be on her level. If love was a need, she'd consider him as a giver.

Femi opened the door, forcing a frown to cover her face.

"When did I give you permission to show up at my place? Especially before noon?"

Ignoring her questions, Asylum stepped into her apartment. He made sure to look her frame over, dark eyes sparkling as he bit back a smile in the process. Inhaling his fresh scent, Femi closed her eyes as she closed and locked the door behind him. She definitely wasn't dressed for company.

Her hair was sitting at the top of her head in a loose, messy bun. Her lips were void of their signature black lipstick. And she was dressed in a matching Ethika sports bra and boy shorts. If it were anyone else, she would have been in a rush to grab her robe before opening the door, but with Asylum... she didn't feel the need.

"Put that gun away," he ordered, standing at the entry hallway, waiting for her.

"What are you doing here, Asylum?"

"You got some food in here? A nigga ain't ate since yesterday."

After looking to the right and left, Asylum headed down the left side of the hall without waiting for her guidance or direction. Groaning under her breath, Femi taped the pistol back under the entryway table and found him seated at her dining room table.

"I'm not a people person, so you need to say whatever the hell you need to say and leave."

Ignoring her, Asylum looked around her apartment. The small studio space was the complete opposite of her mansion back in Peru, but she had grown to like it. Made her feel more grounded. Less lonely.

"I would think you'd be in a mansion somewhere. This is cool, though. The dark décor fits your mean ass."

Gritting her teeth to keep from smiling, Femi slowly stepped in his direction. "It was chosen for me before I got here. I could fit this whole damn apartment in my bedroom back in Peru."

He nodded, eyes scanning the abstract pictures that hung on the wall.

"Why aren't you a people person?" Asylum met her eyes. "You ain't got no people?"

Any other time she'd expressed the lack of her origin family, Femi didn't mind. However, an ounce of shame began to fill her as she thought about discussing that with

Asylum. Unsure of why she wanted to please or impress him, Femi huffed as she headed for the kitchen.

"I was going to make me a smoothie for breakfast. I don't really cook." She shrugged as she opened the refrigerator. "There's some bacon in here and a can of biscuits."

Slowly, Asylum stood and sauntered over to her. He stood behind her – dangerously close. Tightening her grip around the refrigerator handle, Femi snaked her tongue around both lips as her eyes closed. His chest pressed against the back of her, and the moment he inhaled her scent and exhaled against her neck her eyes fluttered.

"You ain't got no people?"

"No," she answered softly, pushing him back and walking away from the refrigerator. "Do you want a smoothie or not?"

He chuckled and leaned against the sink. "Not. I can order us something from Café Venize if you want."

Avoiding his eyes, Femi considered his request. With a curt nod, she headed out of the kitchen. They discussed what he would order when they made it back to the dining room table. To her surprise, he grabbed the bible and immediately turned to Romans.

"You read the bible?"

He nodded, smiling at her softly. "Is that so hard to believe?"

"Hell yea."

"I could say the same about you."

"Touché."

"You mind if I light up?"

Unable to hide her smile, she sat up further in her seat. "Not at all. I smoke when I read the bible sometimes, too. Makes my mind and spirit feel clearer."

"I feel the same way."

For a few seconds, they stared at each other before Asylum cleared his throat and looked away. He pulled the blunt that was nestled carefully behind his ear down and took his lighter from his pocket.

"So why you ain't got no people?"

"Why do you keep asking me that?"

"Clearly because I want to know. Ain't this how normal people have conversations and get to know each other?"

"That's what we're doing now? Getting to know each other?" He remained silent, causing Femi to roll her eyes. "No. I don't have any people. My mother was murdered by my father's enemies at my third birthday party, and he was murdered before I turned eighteen. Tatum was all I had left, but he's an enemy now. So, no, I don't have any people, Asylum."

She expected him to show her pity like everyone else did. As Asylum lit the blunt, he shook his head.

"I never knew my dad, and my mama overdosed in front of me, so I know what it's like to not have any people, too. Bailey and Diego, they're like my family. And Greg took me under his wing after my mama died. I got associates here and there, you know? But I don't know anyone walking around this city with the same blood as me."

He took two puffs, then handed the blunt to Femi. She accepted, wrapping her mind around what they had in common.

"I'll be your person," he offered, following up immediately with, "If you want me to."

It was the first time she'd seen him not display full confidence. Knowing it came from wanting to be connected to her made Femi smile softly.

"Will you expect me to be your person, too?"

Asylum's head tilted as he accepted the blunt from her. "Yea... that's... usually how it works."

After thinking it over for a few seconds, Femi agreed with, "I would like that," quietly. Lowering her head, she tried to hide her smile until Asylum reached across the table and lifted her chin. "Keep ya head up so I can see that smile. I worked hard as hell for that."

Without giving her time to reply, Asylum stood and put his seat next to hers. As they waited for the food, they finished the blunt and read the bible. Femi for sure wasn't expecting Asylum to not only read the bible but understand it and discuss it so fluently. She figured he was the type to only go to church for funerals, so experiencing this side of him definitely had her nose open.

When the food arrived, Asylum finally shared the reason for his impromptu visit. He told her that he wanted to take advantage of her offer. The first assignment he had for her in exchange for association with him was to hook him up with a supplier that would give him two times as strong a strain of weed and cocaine for ten percent less than what he was paying now. It was definitely going to be a challenge, but it was one that Femi would be up for. Besides, she'd been itching to get back in the game, and this would be her first step.

Once she secured herself as his connect, she'd be able to start supplying the Midsouth and beyond.

As much as she was dreading talking to Asylum, she was just as disappointed when it was time for him to leave. She wouldn't dare say that to him, though. Following him slowly to her front door, Femi tried to think of something she could say to make him stick around a little longer. She sucked at small talk, but it didn't matter because Asylum asked...

"What do you desire?" Crossing her arms over her chest, Femi sighed. "Who are you?"

This was the second time he'd asked her that, and just like the first time, she didn't know how to answer him. It would seem silly to admit she had no desires beyond keeping her life and staying in the drug game. And outside of her reputation in the streets, Femi honestly didn't know who she was. Her father groomed her to take his place from a young age, so she didn't spend her time exploring other career options like normal teenagers did. College was a no go, and beyond making money... she didn't really have anything else that she looked forward to on a daily basis.

"Why do you care?" she asked with more aggression than she'd planned to. Dropping her arms, she allowed her shoulders to relax and her winkled brows smoothed out. Flaring her nostrils, she inhaled a deep breath. "Why do you care about me?"

Femi scratched her scalp under her bun as distress began to fill her. She sighed, eyes fluttering as her heart began to palpitate. Every time she was in his presence, he made her feel something she wasn't used to. Yea, he said or did something to piss her off... but there was something else there, too.

Asylum stared down at her intensely, as if the answer to her question was in her own eyes. The heat between them began to intensify. Even without touching her, she felt the magnetic pull he possessed pulling her towards his body. She wanted desperately to feel his arms wrap around her, and Femi could tell he had the same need when he balled his fists and tugged his bottom lip between his teeth as his eyes lowered.

"You playin' a dangerous game lookin' up at me like that, Femi."

Without another word, Asylum turned and left, and as much as Femi wanted more... she was sure his abrupt departure was for the best.

8

Asylum

The last thing Asylum wanted to do as he sat in his car was talk on the phone – business or otherwise. He'd just switched out the flowers on his mother's grave. It took a year for Asylum to save enough money to get her the tombstone he felt she deserved after she died, which was part of the reason he agreed to work for

Greg. Even though his mother struggled with her addiction to crack, she never wanted him to be a part of that lifestyle. Honestly, he had gone as far as he did in the game as a rebellion towards her.

And God.

He was angry with them both for so long because she'd left him.

He was angry at the person who sold his mother that fatal dose of crack, too.

Asylum had vowed to murder the corner boy who was responsible, but Greg never told him who it was.

The ringing stopped, but it started right back up when the caller dialed his line again. Sucking his teeth, Asylum snatched his phone out of the cupholder and groaned at the sight of Miranda's name and picture. He was supposed to make her place his next stop, but he hadn't desired her sexually since meeting Femi. Every time he tried to fuck her, he'd think about Femi – like he was cheating on her or some shit. That had never happened before, and Asylum didn't know how he felt about it.

No matter how hard he tried, denying his attraction for Femi was getting harder and harder.

"Yea?" he answered, starting his car.

"You still coming through?"

Asylum sighed, pinching the space between his nostrils. "Not this evening, Randy. Ion't too much feel like it."

"You're not sick, are you? I can take care of you. And if you're tired, I can put you to bed."

Running his hand down his neck, Asylum closed his eyes and inhaled a deep breath. "I'ma just head home. I'll hit you up tomorrow, though, aight?"

He heard the disappointment deep within her sigh. "Fine. I guess I'll talk to you later."

As his other line beeped, Asylum pulled the phone from his ear to see who was calling. He didn't want it to, but the sight of Femi's name made him smile. "Cool," he agreed quickly before disconnecting the call. "Yea?" he answered, hoping Femi was calling with good news. Even if she wasn't, he would be satisfied just with hearing his voice.

"I have a meeting set up on your behalf, but I don't get good vibes from him. Would you reconsider? My name is hot right now in the streets, all over... I don't trust him, Asylum. But he's the only person willing to hear me out until The Bosses retract the order to blackball me, and we know that's not going to happen."

Asylum released a heavy breath as he ran his hand over his face. "Then we need to make this partnership happen even more. I'll go with you. You ain't got nothin' to worry about. No one will bring you harm as long as you're attached to me." He expected her trust and agreement, but it didn't come easy. "You hear me?"

"Yes."

"That's what you came to me for, right?"

"...Yes."

"So you ain't got nothing to worry about. I got you."

She sighed. "Okay, Asylum. I trust you."

He didn't reply. He didn't move. All he did was sit there, at the cemetery, holding the phone. Listening to her breathe. And he couldn't remember the last time he felt more peace.

Femi

Her leg shook rapidly. Femi had never been one to allow frazzled nerves to consume her. Tonight, she couldn't help herself. As she sat across from Luis, Asylum casually placed his hand on her thigh. Immediately, her leg stopped shaking. Femi looked down at his hand and he pulled it away.

She didn't want him to – which was proof that he needed to.

Luis agreed to meet them at his wife's restaurant, the underground storage unit to be exact. On one half, there were boxes of dry seasonings and supplies. On the other half, there were crates of marijuana. Luis' guards surrounded them, but there was no fear in Femi's heart. Her shaking leg and nerves came from not having complete control of the situation. Before she killed Mateo, she had the drug world in the palm of her hand. There was never a reason for her to seek help from anyone else.

Every time she had to ask someone for something, she felt herself growing weaker and weaker. The concept of relying on a man was foreign to her since her father had been gone for so long. And Luis seemed to be amused by her tight expression and dark eyes because he was in absolutely no rush to speak.

Femi rolled her tongue around her cheek, squeezing her thighs together as she exhaled a hard breath.

"You just gon' sit there and look at us?" she asked, brows bunching together.

Luis smiled and looked in Asylum's direction. "I was trying to get an understanding of what you thought you could accomplish by coming here."

"If you actually communicated that, I could give you an answer."

"You will not disrespect me in my restaurant. My country. You're lucky I even agreed to see you. The Bosses would destroy me if they knew I was in communication with you."

"If that's how you feel, why didn't you say that? I could have stayed home."

Luis tilted his head as he looked at Asylum again.

"Truthfully, I wanted to be in the presence of the woman bold enough to go against The Bosses and still be alive."

A small smile lifted the side of Femi's mouth. She'd become an even greater legend now, but that reputation held no value to her unless she was able to get back in the game. Who gave a fuck if men respected her for going against The Bosses if they were too afraid to help her move weight? If she had to, Femi would grow her own weed and mix her own cocaine, but that would take too long to satisfy Asylum. He wanted a decrease in what he was spending now, and she was in no position to deny him of that.

"Many share your enthusiasm, but few are willing to be just as brave and partner with me." Luis sat back in his seat, running his hand down his beard. "Tatum and I are no longer partners, and I am looking for new suppliers to work with." She looked at Asylum and gestured her hand in his direction. "This is one of my clients. Asylum Marine. I'm sure you're familiar with him. He's a legend in Memphis. Only two men have been able to go against the DEA and cause a citywide shutdown..."

"Your father, one of my oldest friends..."

Clenching her jaw, Femi nodded slowly as she swallowed. "Yes. And you know that shutdown was the reason he left America and stayed here temporarily."

"I should have been more welcoming. Maybe he would have come back here instead of going to Peru only to be murdered as if he was some common man on the street."

She nodded again. Talking about her father was always hard, but she knew comparing Asylum to him would be her best bet.

"Exactly. But Asylum was able to not only avoid jail

time but he has a host of government officials now on his payroll. No man is invincible, but Asylum can be a very profitable client. His reach is vast. He supplies the entire South and he's making his way into the West coast as well. Asylum and his team are easily pulling in seven figures a month, and with your product, I'm sure they can bring in three times as much as they are now. As his reach grows, so will his need, which means he will eventually become one of if not your most consistent customers.

If we can guarantee at minimum five hundred pounds of two of your bestselling strains of weed a month..."

Luis chuckled and shook his head, causing the guards around them to do the same. "You can't move a thousand pounds of weed a month."

"Asylum serves to everyone. Whether it's the nigga in the hood who can't spend more than twenty dollars on an ounce to the judge who requires secret deliveries and pays five hundred an ounce... he has the South on lock. And he's also not the nigga to fuck with. Now, if you're not interested in making this money, I can take his business somewhere else."

Femi stood, but before Asylum could follow suit, Luis was lifting his hand and telling her to wait.

"I can do three a pound."

"One and a half."

"One and a half? Are you out of your mind, Femi?"

"One. Question me again and we're leaving."

She saw the confusion flash across Asylum's face, but it quickly passed. It was risky giving Luis an ultimatum since he was the only supplier returning her phone calls, but she saw his eyes light up when Femi told him Asylum could afford to buy a thousand pounds of weed a month. They hadn't even discussed the cocaine. The power had reversed, and now, it was her job to secure the best deal possible for Asylum. He'd asked for a ten percent increase, but Femi was determined to cut it in half.

Luis looked from her to Asylum as he rubbed his hands together. He took a few seconds to weigh his options, but eventually, he agreed with, "Fine. One thousand a pound, but that's only if he gets a thousand a month. No discount on the cocaine."

Femi

He wouldn't stop staring at her. The whole time she ate, Asylum's eyes wouldn't leave her. He hadn't even eaten his own food because he was too busy taking in every inch of her face. At first, Femi felt awkward and annoyed; now, she couldn't help but blush and think it was cute. It was clear that he was impressed with her negotiation skills, but he hadn't said it aloud yet.

Scratching her ear, Femi slowly chewed the last piece of her smothered chicken before chuckling quietly.

"Are you not going to eat?"

"I asked for ten percent. You got the shit for half of what I pay my current supplier."

"Old supplier," she corrected, nodding towards his plate. "Eat your food, Asylum. We have probably one hour to rest before we have to head to the airport."

With a sigh, Asylum picked up his fork and gently stabbed his now cold cheese and pepper covered chicken.

"Why did you do that?"

Femi thought over his question as she took a sip of her wine-filled margarita. "I wanted to show you what I'm capable of. I don't want you to think helping me puts you in a position to lose. With me, you can prosper and win big." She shrugged. "Guess I just... wanted to make sure you understood that."

Asylum set the fork down on the side of his plate. "What do you desire?"

Femi's head shook as she chuckled and wiped her mouth. "Why do you keep asking me that?"

"Shit, I don't know. I wanna know you."

"But why do those two things make you feel as if you'll know me?"

She counted three Mississippi's before he tilted his head and softly answered her. "Those two questions will tell me everything I need to know about you. Except the shit I'll have to figure out with time."

"Well, I don't know, so you'll have to ask me something else. A normal question. Like what's my favorite color."

"Black. I don't care about that simple shit right now. I'm tryna get to your core."

"Asylum..."

"Tell me about your father." Her eyes squeezed together tightly. "He seems to be the only thing that gets a rise out of you unless I'm pissin' you off." She smiled as her nostrils flared. "Was he as ruthless as legend says he was?"

Slowly, Femi opened her eyes and looked into his. She lifted her glass and drunk as much of the margarita as she could without getting a brain freeze. Normally, she wouldn't have gotten a fruity drink, but with it being as big as it was, and as cheap as it was, Femi couldn't resist.

"He was in his business, to a certain extent. My father had a big heart, though. He took care of his people. I think more people loved him than hated him, which was why his enemies hated him. A part of it was the power and success he possessed, but it was the love, too. Honestly, he was... a lot like you. Ambitious, fearless, feared, respected; he was a lord."

"Is that why you really came to me?"

She didn't answer right away, afraid to admit the truth to herself and to him. With a nod, she slowly lowered her head and grabbed her drink.

Silence found them momentarily and Asylum finally began to eat his food.

"Your mother..." she started, unable to ignore him pause before putting his chicken covered fork into his mouth. "What was her name?"

"Catherine." He smiled as his eyes softened. "Everyone called her Cat. She was..." He paused, looking into the distance as his head shook. "My everything."

Femi's heart dropped as she regretted even asking. If

she had a second nickname, one that at least her father called her, Femi knew his mother – and who killed her. It didn't register the first day Asylum came to her apartment and mentioned Greg. Her father never called him Greg; he called him Grim – because anyone who got on Greg's bad side would end up dead.

Femi remembered it like it was yesterday. She found her father sobbing in his bathroom with an empty bottle of Vodka between his legs. When she asked him what was wrong, he rambled in his drunken state about all the women he loved being taken away from him. First, his Lovey, now... Catty Cake. He said he never should have denied her because he knew she'd go to Grim, but he was praying she'd have more self-control.

"Had she been on drugs your whole life?" She prayed he would have said yes, because that would have meant she wasn't the same woman her father was dealing with.

"Nah. She was hooked by my dad. He was a dealer and she was a good girl gone bad. Daddy issues and all that shit. When she got pregnant with me, she got clean, though. He left, and she had another relapse, but after a rehab stay, she got her shit together." He paused, eyes trailing away from hers. "When I was fourteen, she thought she'd met the man of her dreams." Femi massaged her heart through her chest. "I never met 'em, but he had her head gone. I don't think he was as into her as she was into him. Maybe he was only after her for sex, or he was in love with someone else. Whatever it was, they fucked around for a little over a year before he cut her off. I guess it triggered her and she started using again. That time, she didn't want to go to rehab."

His eyes returned to hers as he licked his lips and swallowed hard. Asylum chuckled. "You know that video of that little boy slapping his mama because she was doing drugs that had everybody up in arms?" Femi nodded. "I had that same kind of moment with my mama. She'd left me at home for three days straight and didn't come home for my birthday. When our next-door neighbor noticed, she came over and got me." His head flung back, eyes went to the ceiling. "Made me a cake and sung me happy birthday. I was so angry with my mother when she came home that night, I started yelling at her and pushed her so hard, she fell. After that, I didn't talk to her for a whole week. I felt like... I couldn't control my anger and I never wanted to disrespect her. Something just... took over me. But my silent treatment made her realize she needed to get help. She promised me she would go to rehab, but before she dropped me off with her friend, she told me she needed one last hit. And that last hit was the one she overdosed on. I often blame myself for not..."

"No, Sy." Reaching across the table, Femi covered his hand with hers. "Don't you dare hold that weight on your shoulders. You were her child. It was not your responsibility to keep her sober."

He sniffed and slowly removed his hand from under hers before standing. "I gotta piss, then I'll be ready to go."

Femi watched as he pulled a few bills out of his pocket and tossed them on the table. Not letting him leave right away, she stood and wrapped her hand around his wrist. Using it to gently pull him in her direction, she watched as a panged expression covered his face.

"Your touch," he muttered, pressing his body into hers. "Femi."

Her eyes fluttered. This wasn't the first time Femi heard her name being spoken, but from his lips, it sounded like a promise to her heart. Or maybe even a warning. Before she could decide which, Asylum was taking her hand into his. She felt the spark ignite between them as heat radiated throughout her entire being.

Femi felt herself began to wilt. To completely weaken against him. Her mind told her to put space between them, but her heart wanted him closer. Wanted him… everywhere.

"Just like that," he whispered, cupping her cheek and using it to tilt her head. "I want you soft. Melting into me like snow in the rain."

Her breath came out shaky as she clutched the hem of his shirt. Lips parted slightly, Femi shook her head as if that would keep the warning bells from blasting louder and louder. From reminding her of her mother's death. And her father's death. And his pain over losing the women he loved. His fear of ever getting close again. How it seeped into her, too. Paralyzing her and making it impossible for her to desire anything beyond sex from a man.

Because she could fall in love, too.

And she could lose, too.

And if she had to bury another person that she loved… Femi honestly didn't know what she would do.

"This is just business," she reminded them both.

With a smile, Asylum released her. "This stopped being business the moment you started lettin' a nigga in."

Asylum

Asylum could tell something was bothering Femi. She was talking, nonstop. Almost as if she was trying to keep her mind from having a moment to settle on whatever was racing around in it. Asylum had continued to entertain her, but as he carried her bags into her apartment, he knew he needed to get down to the bottom of this.

"Who named you?" she asked, nibbling on her thumbnail.

"The streets, I guess."

"So it isn't your birth name?"

"Nah. I got it about five years after I started working with Greg."

He watched her face twist as she grabbed her neck and sat down on the couch.

"Uh—" Her eyes went from him to the picture of her father, Compton, hanging over the fireplace. She said it was the only thing she'd been able to take from Peru when she fled. The original version of the picture was small, six by nine, but she'd had it blown up.

"Will you just tell me what's on your mind, Femi?"

Asylum made his way over to her. Sitting next to Femi, he took her hand into his. He knew she didn't like affection, usually, but she'd been opening up to him. Asylum found it strange that he even desired to be affectionate with her, because he didn't like it himself. The reason his relationship with Miranda worked as well as it did was because she tried to accept him the way he was. There were moments when she'd try to hang around him for too long, kiss all on him, or try to make love – and that was usually when they had their problems.

But with Femi... he wanted those things himself. Not just to receive them, but to give them to her as well. So when she covered his hand on top of hers and looked into his eyes, his breathing stopped. Something sparked between them, some... deep... accepting and understanding... that didn't require any words.

Blinking her eyes rapidly, Femi inhaled a shaky

breath. "I—I don't want to be the one to tell you this." She smiled softly as her eyes watered. "But, I think, too, that I should be the one who tells you."

"Tell me what, Femi? Spit that shit out."

"Just... answer one last question. Did your mother have any other nicknames?" She paused and nibbled on her lap. "Catty Cake, for instance?"

Asylum scratched his temple, then his ear. He ran his hand down his neck as he thought over her question. Catty Cake. At first, he shook his head, but it turned into him nodding as he was filled with recollection.

"She had a gold plated necklace with Catty Cake on it. I assume the nigga she was in love with gave it to her. Nobody called her that, though."

"And you never knew who he was? Not even his name?" Asylum shook his head. Her eyes went back to the picture of her father, and Asylum refused to believe what she was insinuating. "My father... he knew your mother. He's the one who gave her that nickname. And that necklace."

She removed her hands from his and began to pace.

"They were together. Your mother and my father." She paused, giving him time to accept what she'd said. "He told me in the beginning that he didn't want to bring her around because he didn't want me to get attached to another woman who probably wouldn't last in my life. That if they were to get engaged, I would meet her then. But... yea. They were in a relationship for about a year and a half. And I know you think she was with someone who didn't mean her well, but it was the complete opposite.

They were in love. My father was afraid. He was afraid of loving and losing again like with my mother. You know how this life is, our enemies will use anything and anyone to get to us. He didn't want her to be his weakness or a target. So as much as it hurt him to, he broke up with her. He thought he was doing the right thing for them both, but he realized that was the wrong move when she started using again."

Femi stopped pacing and stood in front of him. "She was the reason we went to Peru. That's where he trained, but he never planned to go back. When my mother got pregnant with me and they moved back to the States, that was supposed to be it for us. He was okay with that even after my mother was murdered. Then... your mom. He said there was nothing else for him here, and he didn't want to risk getting attached to anyone else. Losing her... changed him. More than losing my mother did. He became even more heartless and cold. Detached. Focused only on money and business."

She kneeled before him, cupping his cheeks and lifting his head. "Your mother was loved, Asylum. I can promise you that."

His hands covered her wrists. "So... we were almost stepbrother and sister?"

Femi chuckled and nodded. "Almost. And things would be a hell of a little different I'm sure if they would have stayed together."

There was a small piece of Asylum's heart that was filled with peace. It felt good to know that his mother had been loved. Fucked with him to know the lack of that love triggered her in such a way, but he couldn't blame Compton for that. His mother chose to return to the thing that broke her most. That was no one's fault but her own. It took him years to accept that. Hell, he hadn't started to until he talked to Femi about it in Bogotá. Asylum said he'd let it go, but she helped him realize he hadn't released it.

He was still holding on to it.

To her.

But she wouldn't want that for him.

"Compton was a legend. Is a legend. Can't believe my mama had it like that."

Femi smiled, tilting her head slightly to kiss his palm. "There's more." Her smile fell as she inhaled a deep breath. "I know who killed your mother."

Asylum's hands dropped as he sat back on the couch. Femi stood, taking a step back from him. He sat up, elbows on his thighs. Hands covering his mouth. Their eyes locked.

This was the moment he'd been waiting for, for over a decade. Fourteen years, to be exact. Clenching his jaw, Asylum inhaled a deep, steady breath as he waited more patiently than he thought he could for her to speak.

Closing her eyes, Femi ran her hands down her face. When she opened them, she said, "It was Greg."

Asylum's heart twisted. Then stopped. Just to start beating like a wild beast trapped within a cage. His eyebrows began to wrinkle as his mouth dried. Palms and underarms began to sweat. Lowering his hands from his face, his head shook.

"You're wrong."

"No, I'm not. He told my father. He knew my father cared about her because my father told him if he sold her drugs, he'd make him pay. Greg did it anyway. When he gave her that lethal dose, he sent word to my father, pleading for his life. My father told me the only reason he didn't kill him was because her son deserved that honor. Of course, I didn't know it was you until yesterday. But he said that one day you'd find out the truth, and you alone deserved to seek justice on your mother's behalf."

Asylum chuckled as he stood, forcing Femi to take a step back. "So, you're telling me the man that's taught me everything I know is the reason my mother is dead?" She nodded. "That's why he took me in, isn't it? I thought it was because he was trying to be solid, but it's because his ass was guilty. Maybe he wanted to keep me close to make sure I never found out it was him. And if I did, that I wouldn't believe it."

Licking her lips, Femi squeezed the back of her neck.

"Asylum, I'm..." Ignoring her words, he pushed her out of his path gently and headed for the door. "Sy... wait. If you're... I can go with you... You shouldn't be driving right now."

No words were registering in Asylum's brain in order for him to form a response. In that moment, he only had one goal, and that was to finally kill the man responsible for his mother's death.

12

Femi

Femi was conflicted. She wanted to trust that Asylum would be okay, but all she could think about when he left was him needing her and she wouldn't be there. In his right mind, Asylum was unfuckwithable. But he'd just found out the man who had grown to be like a father to him was responsible for his mother's death. How could he remain logical after that?

Six hours had passed, and she wasn't expecting to hear from him at this point. So when he called her and told her to answer the door, Femi damn near leaped out of her bed to let him in. After making a pit stop in the bathroom to look herself over in the mirror and brush her teeth, she quickly headed down the hall to open the door.

As soon as she did, she pulled him into her arms and melted against him.

"I was worried about you. I didn't know if you were going to be walking into a trap or not."

Asylum chuckled against her quietly as he pulled her closer. "No matter how upset I am, I also keep a level head before making any moves. The shit started to fuck with me, though; that's why I came back here."

Releasing him, Femi looked into his eyes. They were red, and she couldn't tell if it was because he'd been crying or because he'd been smoking. She told him to go into her bedroom while she snagged a bottle of Hennessy out of the kitchen. Once she had her custom-made ashtray and two blunts, she headed back to her room where she found Asylum sitting on the edge of her bed.

Femi set the weed and alcohol on the bed, then lowered herself to take off his shoes. Then his pants. Then his shirt. Briefly, she admired his build. His muscles. His tattoos. But only for a moment. This wasn't about sex; this was about his emotional relief.

"Get under the covers," she ordered, using the lighter on her dresser to light a few candles and incense. She pulled up Pandora on her TV and started the Al Green channel before she snuggled up next to him. As he lit the blunt, she poured them both a glass of Hennessy.

"So what happened?"

Femi listened intently as Asylum filled her in. When he first left, his plan was to confront Greg. He wanted to ask him if it was true, why he'd done it, and what his true reason was for taking him under his wing. But when he saw him, words no longer mattered. He knew in his gut that it was true. It's what made the most sense.

Why Greg kept him shielded from the world for the first year after his mother's death. He said it was to train him, but the real reason had finally come out now. Why his wife hated him so much and would often pick fights, begging Greg to get rid of Asylum before he found out the truth. Why Greg didn't work as hard as Asylum felt he should have to find out who was responsible for his mother's overdose. The amount of crack that she'd ingested was no different than the amount she usually used – but it was a bad batch. One that had taken the lives of other addicts as well.

Without a word, Asylum sent three bullets into Greg's skull. As his body dropped, his best friend and two of his bodyguards came rushing in, but it was too late. They were in such disbelief over what they were seeing that Bailey and Diego had time to train their guns on them as Asylum turned in their direction. Greg's best friend, Sonny, confirmed that Greg was the one who'd given Catherine that fatal hit.

She was anxious for her last hit, and Greg was just as greedy then as he was now. Instead of waiting for one of his corner boys to arrive with a few bags of the fresh batch, he gave her one of the bags that were bad and hoped her system was strong enough to fight it. Whether it was or wasn't, he didn't give a fuck. He'd gotten her crinkled-up dollar bills, and that was all he cared about.

Greg wasn't expecting Catherine to snort it in the trap house, though. With her son sitting in the car. As he heard Asylum's cries for his mother, he rushed out to see what was going on, and that's when he immediately decided to hide the truth. Asylum had a reputation of fighting anyone he found selling his mother drugs. He thought one last hit would be okay. That it would hold her over until she made it to rehab. Then, she'd be okay. And their lives would be back to normal.

But as time passed while Asylum waited for his mother in the car, he knew something was wrong. Imagine his surprise when he went into the house and found her slumped over in the corner, foaming at the mouth as her body shook and eyes rolled into the back of her head.

"I told them that since I'd taken him out, by street law, they work for me now. Bailey's in the process of setting up meetings with his suppliers, workers, and money men now."

"So you're going to run his business and yours? Can you handle that?"

Asylum shrugged as he swirled the Hennessy around his glass. "Ain't nothing I can't handle. More money will bring more problems, but I'll cross that bridge when I get to it."

"Well... you know I'll help you in any way that I can."

Asylum smiled as he cut his eyes at her. "Of course you will. Your ass been waiting for ways back in."

"No, I'm serious! A part of me feels like I owe this to you. I know my father wasn't responsible for the choice she made, but... I still feel bad. So whatever you need, I got you."

He nodded, putting his glass on the nightstand by her bed. "I 'preciate that."

"So how do you feel? Relieved? Do you feel worst because you trusted him?"

"I thought I would feel bad because of how close we were, but that shit meant nothing to me in that moment. Not when it comes down to my mama. He became nothing to me the moment you told me that. Knowing who was responsible definitely filled me with a sense of peace. I feel like I can finally let her go now and let her rest."

Femi smiled and ran her hand down the back of his neck. "Good. That makes me happy."

Asylum licked his lips as he stared into her eyes. "You know what makes me happy?" Her head shook. "You."

Lowering her head, Femi blushed. Things were definitely changing between them, but they'd yet to acknowledge it. Not beyond the restaurant conversation they had yesterday.

"Yea?" she confirmed softly, lifting her eyes back to his.

"Hell yea."

Sliding her hand from the back of his neck to his cheek, Femi confessed, "You make me happy, too."

Asylum put the ashtray and bottle of Hennessy on the nightstand, appearing to need now more than ever to be inside of her. To be one with her. To connect with her and get to know her in a way that he'd never known a woman before.

Their faces slowly began to gravitate towards one another, but neither made the first move. Hell, neither had ever been into kissing and making love. Taking the lead, Femi softly pressed her lips against his. She did it a second time, keeping her eyes locked with his.

"Asy–"

Before she could ask him if that was okay, he showed her that it was by using her hair to pull her lips back to his. This time, she closed her eyes as Asylum deepened the kiss. A quiet moan escaped her lips when he lifted her and placed her on his lap. Slowly, his tongue slipped inside of her mouth. With two handfuls of her ass, Asylum kissed her with so much passion and tenderness, she wanted to cry out to God and thank Him for allowing Asylum to reserve all of this for her.

As his lips trailed down her cheek and neck, Asylum pushed her panties to the side. She busied herself with pulling him out of his boxers while he pushed the cups of her bra down and alternated between nibbling and licking her nipples.

Sliding down onto his hardened shaft, Femi's head flung back as she inhaled a deep breath. She squeezed the back of his neck as their eyes locked. Slowly, she rode him, losing herself in this moment. In his eyes. His kisses. His hands. The feel of his dick stretching her and making her his. Femi may have come to Asylum seeking the meaning of his name… but she was no longer able to deny the fact that he was giving her the meaning of hers now, too.

Asylum

Life had been going in a direction that neither Asylum nor Femi had expected, but they were surprisingly prepared for it. After they made love, things changed drastically. While neither of them felt compelled to put a title on what they had, they'd been spending every night together. The agreement he had with Miranda had been canceled, and to his surprise, she didn't give him much slack about it. Could have been because she expected him to come back to her as he always did. Whatever the case, all of his free time was being spent with Femi.

Tonight, they were going on their first real date. They both were in need of a distraction after their first shipment from Luis was delivered with a note – Tatum knows. At first, Femi's paranoia had her convinced that they needed to get rid of the shipment because Tatum had somehow convinced Luis to let him track it. But it didn't matter to Asylum. Whether Tatum knew where he'd had the delivery sent or not, he wasn't bold enough to come and confront him.

Not by himself at least.

And from what Femi had told him, their men didn't move off Tatum's orders; they moved off Femi's orders. None of them would come with him to bring her back. They did, however, have to consider if The Bosses would lend him their men to build a team. If they did, Asylum would be prepared – even more so now. It was one thing for him to be helping Femi as a favor to Rule and Camryn. Now, he was doing it because he felt responsible for her. The moment he gave her his heart, he dedicated himself to keeping it safe inside of her.

"I can't believe you gave Rule such a hard time."

Asylum smiled as he switched the phone from his right ear to the left. He should have known Camryn was going to fill her in on their conversation. After the delivery was made and he discussed all possible outcomes with Femi, Asylum went to pay Rule a visit. In that moment, he was angry. Not just because he'd gotten him to agree to help Femi, but because he'd fallen for her. He blamed Rule for bringing her into his life, and Rule knew immediately it was because he was catching feelings for her.

What was supposed to be an opportunity for him to let off some steam and worry turned into him bearing his soul about how fucked up he'd be if he couldn't protect Femi and something happened to her. In that moment, he felt like the helpless sixteen-year-old boy who held his mother as her spirit surrendered to God. But Rule didn't allow him to stay in that moment for too long.

Yes, Rule ran the streets. So did Camryn. But they both went legit when they decided to get married. Rule went to school to become a therapist, and he ended up giving Asylum exactly what he needed in that moment.

"I bet Camryn couldn't wait to call you with her nosey ass."

Femi chuckled. "You know she couldn't. How far away are you?"

"'Bout ten minutes away."

"Okay, cool. I'll see you when you get here. I need to finish getting ready."

"Aight."

After Asylum disconnected the call, he returned his attention back to the road ahead. Absently, he massaged the center of his chest where the tattoo of his mother's face was. Finally knowing who was responsible for her death had given him great relief. When he thought of her now, he wasn't filled with anger or sadness. Now, he felt numb. Not happy, but not sad, either. That was a start.

Seven minutes later, Asylum was pulling into his usual parking space in front of her apartment. They'd been spending so much time together, he was tempted to tell her to move in with him. It wasn't as if he didn't have the space. Even if she didn't want to be in his room, he had more than enough for her to have her own.

Femi was too independent for that, though. Right now at least. And Asylum could accept that. This was still new for him, too.

When Asylum knocked on her door, he wasn't expecting what he saw when she opened it. Her hair was in loose curls instead of its usual bun. No sunglasses covered her green eyes. And her lips were covered in red lipstick instead of black. Femi was dressed in a silk red robe that was open, exposing the red lace bra and panty set she wore underneath.

Asylum hadn't even noticed the glass of wine in her hand until she giggled and held it out further for him to take.

"You like what you see?"

"Hell yea." Taking the glass from her hand, Asylum wrapped his arm around her and pulled her close. "You look good as fuck, Femi. We stayin' in tonight?"

With a smile, she gripped his arm as his lips kissed up her neck. "Yes. Is that okay? I know tonight was supposed to be our first date outside of our homes, but after how it started, I kind of just want you all to myself. Plus, with you taking over Greg's business, I know we're going to have less and less time to spend together."

"Nah. You're wrong about that. I'll never let business keep me from giving you what you need. I don't have to hide what I do from you because you do it, too, so you will always have access to me."

Her smile widened as she gently tugged him into her apartment. Asylum's nostrils widened as he took in the scent of soul food permeating the air. Last he knew, Femi could barely cook and had no desire to learn.

"You got something delivered?"

"Nah. Um... Camryn gave me a few recipes. I wanted to fix you a homecooked meal since you tried to play me about my different kinds and brands of noodles."

Asylum couldn't help but chuckle as he locked the door behind them. Femi barely ate as she should. Before she came to America, her life consisted of long workdays. At most, she kept full off snacks, noodles, and smoothies. Very rarely did she have a homecooked meal, and if she did, it was fixed by her housekeeper.

"Awww, you learning how to cook for me? I feel special."

Femi rolled her eyes as he pulled her close from behind. "Don't make a big deal out of this. I just figured we could spend the night chilling. Watch a few episodes of *Grey's Anatomy* since that's all you're watching right now."

That was true. He'd been obsessed with the show ever since he started watching it six months ago. Not a lot of people knew it, but if Asylum would have gone to college, it would have been to become a doctor. Since that dream of his life would never become a reality, he lived it through the shows he watched.

"How you expect me to not make a big deal out of this?" Asylum turned her in his arms. "You're cooking for me and you don't even do it for yourself. I'd rather have this over a meal in a restaurant any day. Especially if you gon' serve it to me in this."

His hand wrapped around the front of her neck, tilting her head back. Femi's eyes lowered as she bit down on her bottom lip, wrapping her arms around him. Lowering himself to her, Asylum allowed his tongue to slowly slither its way inside her mouth. As much as he wanted to kiss her and make love to her, he knew they wouldn't be eating any time soon. So, he released her, repositioning himself in his boxers as his dick hardened even more.

He followed her into the kitchen, where he rubbed his hands together at the sight of what she was cooking. Collard greens, candied yams, baked macaroni and cheese, and baked chicken.

"Cornbread?" he asked, figuring there had to be *something* that she'd left out.

"Yep. And your sweet-ass Kool-Aid is in the refrigerator."

Asylum moaned deep within his throat. "You tryna make a nigga marry you, huh?"

She didn't answer as she lifted the top from her greens and gave them a stir.

"Dinner will be ready when the cornbread is."

Happy with his dismissal, Asylum made his way to the dining room table and made himself comfortable. Since she was doing something special for him, he wanted to do something special for her as well. After placing an order for every flavor of popcorn on the Funky Chunky site and having it shipped to her address, he opened a private browser and looked up videos on pussy eating on Pornhub. Up until now, he'd never been ashamed of the fact that he only had sex doggy style or in the dark to avoid the intimacy of looking in a woman's eyes. And as much as he received head, he'd never had a reason to give it.

No woman ever made him want to.

And he could make them come repeatedly with his fingers and thick, ten-inch dick.

But... there was something about Femi. Something

that had him craving the feeling of her lips against his, wanting to slowly stroke her while he stared into her eyes, and desiring to learn how to eat her pussy until she begged him to stop.

Asylum didn't realize how long he'd been watching the videos until she stood behind him, asking, "You taking notes?" Jumping up from his seat, Asylum quickly slammed his phone down on the table. Femi held her stomach and she doubled over in laughter. "The hell you so shaky for?"

"Yo' daddy ain't teach you not to sneak up on a nigga like that?"

She was still laughing so hard, tears were forming in her eyes. As startled and irritated as he was, the sight of her having such a good laugh at his expense calmed him down.

"He did, but that didn't include walking up on my man watching porn."

When she realized what she said, her laughter immediately died down. The tension was thick between them as they stared at each other in silence. Femi was the first to move. She walked along the side of him and placed the cornbread on the table. As she tried to walk away, Asylum gently grabbed her arm and pulled her into his chest.

"What you runnin' for?" he asked with a low voice, though he already knew the answer.

"I didn't mean that."

"Mean what?"

Femi stared into his eyes, gauging his seriousness. "You're really going to make me repeat it?" He nodded. "That you were my man. I didn't mean that."

"So I'm not?"

Her head shook. "No. We said we weren't doing that. Right?" He nodded. "So, no."

"But what if I wanna be?"

"Do you?"

He did, but he couldn't pull himself to say it. Instead, he changed the subject. "I wasn't watching the shit just for the sake of watching it. I was trying to see what to do."

Femi's smile returned. "When do I get to see, well, feel, what you've learned?"

Licking his lips, Asylum wrapped his free arm around her as well. "As far as I'm concerned, you can feed me that pussy right after dinner."

Having heard enough, Femi removed herself from his embrace and quickly went back into the kitchen. She returned not long after with their plates and switched his wine out for the now cold Kool-Aid. For it to have been her first time cooking, she did a damn good job – and Asylum didn't play about his soul food. As much as he wanted to savor the meal and what it meant between them, he was more anxious to savor her.

The moment they were done eating, Asylum stood and carried their plates to the kitchen. Femi was right behind them with their glasses, giggling under her breath. Instead of allowing her to go to her bed, Asylum took her by the hand and placed her on top of the table. Sitting down, Asylum pulled her to the edge of the table and tossed her legs over his shoulders. He pushed her panties to the side, inhaled her scent, then swiped his tongue between her folds.

They both released a quiet moan together...

Femi

Camryn had become the first real adult female friend Femi had ever had. Though she was still getting used to her affectionate ways, chipper attitude, stubborn need to have everything her way, and desire to speak to Femi on a regular basis… Femi would be lying if she said she wasn't enjoying having Camryn in her life.

This afternoon, they agreed to meet up for lunch. Initially, Femi thought it was because something was wrong, but all Camryn wanted to do was have girl talk and catch up. If anyone would have told Femi that her lunch would be spent talking about life and love instead of counting kilos of cocaine…

"That's so sweet," Camryn complimented with a smile. Her curly, natural hair was thick and large, framing her round face perfectly. She had slanted gray eyes and a cute, small nose that made Femi want to pinch it and play keep away. Looking at Camryn, you wouldn't have expected her to be moving the amount of weight she used to move on Anthony's behalf back in the day. But that was the problem their enemies faced – thinking their femininity and beauty were signs of weakness.

"You think everything is sweet," Femi teased, putting her straw between her lips to hide her smile.

"It is! You went from not wanting to deal with a man on a personal level to needing Asylum for peaceful nights of sleep. You yourself said you haven't been having any nightmares since you two started sleeping together. When are you moving in?"

Femi's eyes rolled as she shook her head and smiled. "I'm not moving in. We're not in a relationship."

"Umhm."

"I'm serious, Cam! And it's going to stay that way. Asylum and I are too invested in our businesses for anything serious. My stay here is temporary. When I rebuild and establish myself apart from The Bosses, I'll be leaving Memphis. So… no."

"Does Asylum know you don't plan to be here permanently?"

Twisting her mouth to the side, Femi rolled her

tongue across her cheek. "Yea, I guess. I mean... I'm sure he does."

"Have you actually said those words to him?"

"Well, no."

"So how are you sure you're both on the same page? What are you going to do if that's what he wants? If he wants a future with you? Realistically, you two are perfect for each other because you're both in the business. That might be a reason to part ways to you, but to him, it could be the reason you stay together forever."

Honestly, she and Asylum hadn't talked about the future. When their relationship status came up, one of them would always change the subject. Neither of them wanted things to be personal, but when it did, they never officially discussed it. With the success of their partnership with Luis, Femi was confident that she could move freely within a year and not have to feel as if there was a target on her back. Whether she went to Miami, Jamaica, Bogotá, or beyond... Femi didn't see herself planting her roots in Memphis.

Or Peru for that matter.

Both places had given her a lot, but they'd taken a lot, too. Now, she was ready to start somewhere new.

"I guess that's something we need to sit down and talk about. Asylum isn't the getting married and settling down type, but people do change. Is that something you always wanted?"

Camryn chuckled. "Not at all. Rule did, but I didn't. I held on to my pain and my mother's pain for so long that I was scared of loving and being loved. But Rule... Rule loved that pain out of me." She smiled, and as Femi watched her eyes glisten, she wondered how it felt to be loved that way. "I was you – broken, hurting, angry. Using business to keep from falling in love. And for quite some time, it worked, but when the man that is meant to love you comes along... there's really nothing you can do to stop it."

That might not have been what Femi wanted to hear, but she knew it was true. Her father had the same experience. When he met her mother, Compton was learning from the best in the game to become the best in the game. The last thing he wanted to do in that moment was be blinded by love but he had no choice. And as much as he avoided it, losing her mother scarred him deeper than anything else ever had.

"Maybe that's true. All I know is, we've both loved and lost... and we have nothing more to lose. I refuse to give him too great of a place in my life because I don't have any more space in my heart for holes. If I love him and something happens to him... to us..."

Not even able to stomach the thought, Femi's head shook as she lifted her white wine and gulped it down. Camryn's eyes lifted, gaining Femi's attention. She turned, watching as an unfamiliar man walked past their table and dropped an envelope onto it. They both went from looking at it to each other. Neither was in a rush to pick it up.

Unable to resist, Femi picked up the envelope and opened it. The small piece of paper inside was blank. She turned it over, trying to see if she'd missed anything.

"That's odd. He's clearly trying to send us a message. I'm going to follow him."

"Wait." Camryn reached across the table. Putting the paper to her nose, she closed her eyes and inhaled the scent of it deeply. Her chuckle turned into a brief sob, but she didn't let any tears fall. "It's... Chanel No5. He sprayed this with Chanel No5."

"Okay... what does that mean?"

Camryn's hand trembled as she set the paper down on the table. "This is Anthony. This is his way of sending me a message."

15

Femi

"Okay, make this make sense," Femi ordered.

They'd made it back to Rule and Camryn's home, and she was trying to understand why a blank piece of paper made Camryn believe that Anthony was not only alive, but in Memphis, trying to send her messages.

"Chanel No5. It's significant to us. He used to buy it for my mother and get on me when I tried to wear it because it was too grown-up of a scent. Eventually, he bought me my very first bottle." With a sigh, she stopped pacing and sat next to Femi. "I know this might sound crazy, but Anthony used to have his men watching over me when he was on the run. When he needed to get in touch with me, he did so through them. I'm sure this is his way of doing so now."

"But that doesn't make sense, Cam. He's dead. We buried him. Are you sure you're not trying to make this into something you want it to be? Or could someone be trying to make you think it's Anthony to set us up? Does anyone else know about the perfume besides the two of you?"

Her head shook as she smiled, eyes watering again. "No. Just Rule. And he wouldn't play with my emotions like this. It's Anthony. It has to be. He's alive."

"But we buried him..."

"We buried a body that *looked* like him. For all we know, it could have been a fake. Plastic! Or whatever the hell they use in those damn wax museums!"

Scratching her ear, Femi stood and walked over to the window. Peering out, she wondered how long it was going to take Rule and Asylum to meet them there. If she talked to Camryn for too long, she would probably be able to convince her that her bullshit ass belief was real.

Because the truth was, Anthony was meeting with an FBI agent to give him information on Mateo to secure his freedom. The truth was, if Anthony snitched, he would have been free from the law, but he'd have a target on his back in the streets. The truth was, he'd have to answer to The Bosses the moment Mateo was arrested. If he had any chance of surviving, he'd have to fake his death and take on a new identity to even be able to enjoy his freedom. The truth was... no one actually saw Anthony right after he was shot... so if he wanted to fake his death... he could.

"I don't know, Cam. Do people do this faking their death shit in real life?"

Camryn chuckled. "Well, he'd spent so much of his life on the run. I suspect he'd do just about anything if that meant..."

She continued to talk, but the words were no longer registering in Femi's ears. Not at the sight of the black on black car pulling into the driveway. Not at the sight of Jeremy, Anthony's best friend, getting out. Not at the sight of the passenger door opening... and Anthony getting out. Gasping, Femi clutched her chest as her knees almost gave out on her. She felt like she was looking at a ghost.

Leaning against the window, she softly called Camryn's name. Camryn quickly made it to her side, crying out at the sight of Anthony. Immediately, she rushed to the door and ran outside, jumping into Anthony's arms. She hugged him tight, held him close as he carried her inside. The sound of Camryn's sobbing got louder and louder as Femi stood there – frozen.

Her excitement at seeing him began to dissolve by the time they'd made it in the house. She jumped down from his embrace and smacked him so hard, the sound echoed throughout the room.

"You're supposed to be dead!" she yelled before smacking him again. "I grieved for you! I buried you! You're supposed to be dead!"

Anthony's head hung before he looked in Femi's

direction. "I planned to let you believe that for the rest of my life, but when I heard Femi killed Mateo, I knew I had to come home to fix this. When I was planning to keep you from doing the same thing, I didn't think about having to keep her from going after him. But I should have, knowing especially that you two would be conversing and planting seeds in each other's heads." He took a step in Femi's direction but she held her hands up. "I'm sorry, Femi. I didn't mean for any of this to happen. My hope was that no one would seek to avenge my death so I could live the rest of my life in peace. Now you have a target on your back because of me. But I... I can fix this. I can't go to The Bosses on your behalf, but I can help you figure out how to get back in their good graces."

"I can't believe you're really here," Camryn almost whispered, stepping closer to him. As she cupped his cheek and stared into his eyes, Femi turned her back to all three of them.

All she could think about was the fact that Anthony was like a Godfather to her. She'd grieved for him, too. Lost him, too. Loved him, too. Put her life on the line to place honor behind his. And here he was... standing here apologizing as if what he'd done was something simple and repairable with words.

Her heart began to burn as it beat rapidly. So rapidly, she heard it beating within her ears. It drowned out the voices around her. As her fists opened and closed, she tried to inhale calming breaths. Rule swerved into the driveway just as Camryn made her way to Femi's side. She felt Camryn touching her, but as she looked into her eyes, she couldn't hear anything she was saying.

As if she was no longer in control of her own body, Femi turned and pulled her gun from her waist. She aimed it at Anthony, but as her finger squeezed the trigger, Camryn raised it in the air, sending the bullet through the ceiling. Camryn pushed Femi into the window and tried unsuccessfully to remove the gun from her hand. Kneeing Camryn in the stomach, she aimed at Anthony again just as Jeremy was able to wrap her in a bear hug. As she yelled for him to release her, Femi leaned forward, almost lifting him onto her back.

One last time, she lifted her arm and tried to shoot... but by the time she realized Camryn was now standing in front of Anthony... it was too late.

"No," Anthony yelled, taking Camryn into his arms before her body could hit the ground.

"The fuck is going on?" Rule yelled as both he and Jeremy ran over to Camryn.

As Rule took her from his arms and yelled for someone to call 911, Anthony stood and charged towards Femi... giving her a clear opening to send three bullets into his chest.

Asylum

He'd always known Femi was a beast, but even Asylum couldn't believe what had happened. He arrived shortly after Rule did. Upon entry, his eyes... Asylum was sure they were playing tricks on him. As Camryn coughed up blood, Anthony laid motionless in a puddle of his own. Hospitals were usually off-limits for people in their lifestyle, but they knew if they didn't get Camryn to a hospital soon, she would bleed to death.

Thankfully, Asylum had five doctors on his payroll, and they understood they were not allowed to call the police and report the shooting. As Rule waited at the hospital with his brother and sister-in-law, Power and Elle, Asylum made sure their home was cleaned thoroughly and that Anthony's body was disposed of.

When he was done, he stopped by the hospital to check on Camryn before making his way to Femi's place. At first, she remained silent. A whole two hours had passed before she finally muttered, "I gave up my life, my business, for him, and he wasn't even dead."

Asylum tightened the grip he had on her, kissing her forehead in the process. Her head rested on his chest, using his heartbeat as a melody to calm her soul.

"This shit is fucked up. I don't blame you for taking his ass out. Just as he reached out to Camryn, he should have reached out to you, too. Anthony knew better than anyone what you were capable of doing."

She sniffled, and the thought of her crying was enough to have his own eyes watering. Femi was one of the strongest women he knew, and it fucked with him to know that she was hurting. As her tears coated his skin, Asylum tried to lift her up, but she held him tighter.

"Just makes me feel like we weren't as close as I thought we were. I mean... I loved him like a second father, and he didn't love me enough to show the same care he showed her."

"Baby..." Asylum's voice was strained. "I don't think that's what it was at all. He does, did, love you. If he didn't, he wouldn't have come back. I think he just...

maybe thought *you* didn't love *him* enough to do something like this. Otherwise, I'm sure he would have reached out to you just as he'd done to her to make sure she didn't try to get at Mateo."

"That only makes it worse," she whined. "I killed him, Asylum. He's gone for real now, and it's my fault."

"No. It's his fault. He should have handled this situation differently. You're known for your temper and refusal to deal with betrayal and disrespect. I can't think of too many things more disrespectful than to give up your freedom for a nigga who wasn't even dead because you thought he was."

Femi remained silent, and Asylum hoped it was because she was taking his words in as truth.

"Is Camryn okay? I'm pretty sure I just lost the only friend I had. It was an accident shooting her, but she probably won't want to have anything to do with me now."

"Camryn is a G. She's taken a bullet before. She actually asked for you, but I told her it was best if y'all took a little space from each other. It wasn't you shooting her that fucked with her; it was finding out that Anthony was dead."

Femi sighed. "She has to grieve him all over again after being filled with joy over having him back. I took him from her. Again. Now I'm going to be alone all over again."

Asylum knew better than to take her words personally. He also knew Camryn was offering Femi something that he never could – a connection with a woman that she'd probably never had before.

"You got me."

Looking up finally, Femi met his eyes. "Do I? Because

we agreed this wasn't serious or permanent. Eventually, I'm going to find a way to clear my name and leave Memphis. Then what?"

"Femi, I don't give a fuck about that. If I've learned anything, it's to live in and embrace right now. And right now, you got me, and I got you. That's all the fuck that matters. We'll deal with that other shit when it gets here. You understand me?"

Femi smiled as she gave him a soft nod.

"You always trying to put me in my place," she teased, straddling him fully.

"Nah..." Asylum flipped her over. "I'm always trying to remind you of your place with me."

Her hands went to his chest as she wrapped her legs around him. Just the thought of having him inside of her had Femi's pussy leaking, but she wouldn't rush the sex. Not right now. Right now, his words were providing all the pleasure she needed.

"What place is that?"

Asylum lowered himself to kiss her. "At my side." He kissed her again. "In my heart." Again. "Attached to my soul." And again. "Always on my mind." This time when he kissed her, Femi wrapped her hand around the back of his neck and kept him from getting back up.

Their kisses deepened as his hands began to roam her body. By the time they made it between her legs, she was soaking wet. Asylum moaned into her mouth as he slowly slid inside of her. Breaking their kiss, Femi's lips parted as she inhaled a deep breath. Asylum didn't seem to mind. He nibbled on her bottom lip as he continued to stroke her with the slow, deep pace that they'd both come to crave.

Femi

It took two months. Two months for Camryn to agree to see Femi. Both Asylum and Rule tried to come along, but both ladies decided against it. They met at their usual spot for lunch, and Femi had no idea how their meeting would end. For the first few minutes, they sat in silence, looking at everything but each other. It wasn't until the boneless wings and nachos they ordered arrived that Camryn broke the silence with...

"I was angry because I'd just gotten him back, and you took him from me." Licking her lips, she turned her head and met Femi's eyes. "But honestly, if the roles were reversed, my reaction would have been the same. Anthony hasn't been active consistently in my life... since I was a child, and I shouldn't have expected that to change this time around." Her breath came out shaky. "I was angry at him, too, for making me think he was dead, and it was easier to project that onto you because he was gone. Again. And I had to accept the fact that he's always left me when I need him most. Me and my mother. So..." She reached her hand across the table, waiting for Femi to put her hand inside. "You don't need it, but I offer you my forgiveness – not for you, but for me. Because that's the only way I'll be able to release this. And whether you want to stay in Memphis or not, I want you to be my newest forever friend."

Caressing Camryn's hand with her thumb, Femi smiled. "I would like for you to be my forever friend, too."

Though she didn't really believe in forever these days.

But that was a conversation for another day.

With a squeal, Camryn stood from her seat and walked over to Femi's side to give her a hug. This time, Femi hugged her back just as tightly, happy that they were able to resolve their issue and return to their budding friendship.

As they ate, they caught up on the past two months of their lives. While Femi and Asylum were getting deeper and deeper in the drug game, Camryn and Rule were considering expanding their family and having a third child. Being a mother had never been a desire of Femi's, but as Camryn talked, Femi found herself placing her hand on her stomach, wondering what it would feel like to have a baby in there.

When their lunch was over, they split the bill, and Camryn was the first to leave. As Femi remained at the table, she called Asylum to see where he was and what time he'd be heading home, if at all. Controlling his territory along with Greg's had proven to be more than Asylum thought it would be. Between him, Bailey, and Diego, they were handling it pretty well, but he was definitely being stretched thin.

Femi offered to take over as much territory as he needed her to, and he was considering it, but Asylum didn't want them to have even less time apart.

"What do you desire?" was how Asylum answered, getting an immediate smile out of Femi. "Who are you, Femi?"

"Babe, where are you?"

"Making some runs. Probably won't come to your place and crash until the sun's about to come up."

"Can I meet you and ride with you?"

"You know you don't have to ask."

Tugging her bottom lip between her teeth as she smiled, Femi's grip loosened on her phone. The energy in the restaurant shifted around her immediately. Looking up, her eyes landed on Tatum as he casually entered through the door on the side by her table.

This was the moment she'd been waiting for, and now that it was finally here, a part of her felt relief.

"Hey, Sy?" she called softly as Tatum sat in the chair across from her.

"What's up?"

"I just... I want you to know..." Closing her eyes, she

inhaled a deep breath. "You've made me happier in less than six months than I've been my entire adult life." Smiling, she lowered her head, wanting to avoid Tatum's intrusion in their moment. "When my father died, I didn't think I'd ever find peace and happiness again, but I've found both now that I've gotten to experience you. I guess what I'm trying to say is... I love you."

Asylum released a shaky breath. "Damn, bae. I wish you woulda said that in a nigga's face so I could show you how much I love you, too."

She wanted to tell him that now, he'd probably never have the chance to, but she couldn't do that and send off any alarms. Wouldn't do either of them any good. By the time Asylum made it to her, they'd be gone. Now, she was regretting not allowing him to put bodyguards on her consistently.

"Why don't you just say it now and show me later?"

"I love you, too. And I know you don't want to do the marriage and family thang... but I want you to know next time I see you, I'm putting a baby in you."

Femi giggled as she nodded, trying not to cry. Not because she was scared of her future, but because she wasn't going to be able to have one with Asylum.

"I'm going to hold you to that."

"Don't say that. I'll cancel all this drug shit and pull up on you right now."

Her hand covered her forehead. Mouth opened partially as her heart murmured a steady echo of his name.

"You're telling me you'd give up your empire for me?"

"For us and our chance to live a normal life... the life we deserve? In a muhfuckin' heartbeat."

Finally, Femi opened her eyes. Swallowing hard, she

searched Tatum's eyes... trying to find something that gave way to the man she met when she was six years old. She found nothing.

"Asylum?"

"Yea, baby?"

"Tatum is here."

"Where? With you?" She nodded, forgetting he couldn't see her. "Send me your location."

Smiling, Femi shook her head. "It won't do you any good. Just... promise me that you'll stay safe, okay? And... and don't forget about me. Okay? I love you."

"Femi, tell me where you ar—"

After disconnecting the call, Femi powered her phone off. She quickly wiped away a tear before Tatum could see it. Confusion covered his face as he sat up in his seat.

"Are you... are you crying? The fuck has happened to you, Femi?"

She didn't plan on answering him, and it didn't matter if she wanted to anyway. The waitress casually walking to their table and sticking a needle in the side of her neck caught her completely off guard. Femi was so surprised, she didn't react right away, but as soon as the woman pulled the needle out of her neck and tried to walk away, Femi stood, grabbed her by the back of the neck, and slammed the side of her face onto the table.

"Did you just shoot something in me, bitch? I will fucking break your neck!"

"Femi," Tatum called softly. "Release her. I paid her to do that. Don't make a scene."

Ignoring his words, Femi's grip around the woman's neck tightened as she whimpered.

"Femi," he repeated, louder this time. "Let her go."

Femi released her, and she wasted no time running off.

"What the fuck did you have her stick me with?"

"Relax. It's a sleep aid that's going to knock you out for a few of hours. It's harmless, but I will be using it until we make it back to keep you knocked out." He said it casually, and his nonchalant tone only pissed Femi off more. As her legs began to shake under the table, she looked around the restaurant and weighed her options. "You could try to make a run for it, but that shot is going to knock you out in less than five minutes. The Bosses know I'm here to get you, so if you were able to kill me, they will send their entire army here to get you. And you know what happens if they have to do any extra work – everyone will be murdered that is attached to you. So if you really love that man, you know the only way to keep him safe is to leave with me willingly."

"Did Camryn set me up?"

"What?"

"Did she tell you we would be here?"

"No. I've been following the both of you. After the shooting, I knew she'd meet up with you, and I figured that would be the best time to get you." Their eyes remained locked until he checked the time on his phone. "Four minutes, Femi. Please don't make this hard."

"After everything my father did for you." Tatum rolled his eyes and sat back in his seat. "This is how you repay him?"

"This ain't got shit to do with your father," he gritted. "Or you. You left me in Peru to fend for myself. I became a target, too, so what the fuck did you expect me to do?"

"You were like my brother, Tatum..."

"And I will always love you, but if the choice is me or

you... you know who I'm going to choose. If I don't deliver you, I'm as good as dead, Femi."

Her head shook rapidly. "No, it doesn't have to be that way. Asylum can protect you. Just like he's been protecting me. We can work something out with The Bosses. I'm sure me killing Anthony can add weight to my name with them again."

Tatum shook his head. "No. I'm not willing to risk going against them for you. We gotta go." He stood and looked down at her. "Let's go, Femi."

"Are you sure this is what you want to do, Tatum?"

"Three minutes."

Slowly, Femi stood from her seat. She followed Tatum outside, jerking her arm away from him when he tried to wrap his hand around it. After he opened the door for her, she looked his entire frame over before spitting in his face and slapping him. As much as she wanted to pull her gun and end his life herself, she knew what he'd said was true. If she put up a fight, The Bosses would come to America to get her personally, and if they did, they wouldn't leave until they painted the entire city of Memphis red.

Femi

Her pain was so poignant, it woke her up from her sleep. Groans immediately began to pour from her, but they stopped when her center filled with sharped pains. Inhaling short, choppy breaths, Femi slowly allowed her eyes to flutter open. It didn't surprise her that her eyes landed on Tatum, but he was too busy staring at his phone to notice her.

Taking in her surroundings, Femi knew exactly where she was. She was being held in one of The Bosses' cages, and Tatum of all people was her watchman. The white walls around her had been covered over the years with so much blood, dirt, and feces that they were stained and enough of a disturbing sight to have her stomach feeling queasy.

Her eyes were filled with the sound of the other prisoners in different cages as they yelled, cried, and talked to themselves.

Femi tried to sit up, and that's when she noticed one of her wrists were chained down. Resting on her elbow, she cried out in pain. Were some of her ribs bruised? Laying flat on her back, she closed her eyes and tried to regulate her breathing.

"I tried to convince them not to beat you, especially since you were still asleep, but they didn't listen."

She opened her eyes but didn't bother looking at him.

"You expect me to thank you for that?"

Tatum sighed and moved closer to her. "I'm sorry, okay? Watching what they did to you... it made this shit real. I could handle betraying you in my mind, but it's real now. I can't go through with this, Femi."

Slowly, her head tilted in his direction. "Then uncuff me and let me go."

His head shook as he scratched it. "I can't do that, either. They will kill me."

"Asylum will kill you," she screamed, regretting it as soon as pain seared through her.

"After you meet with The Bosses in two days, they are going to command your punishment from my hands since

I'm the closest person to you. If you have anything up your sleeve to keep that from happening, you have until six p.m. Wednesday to make it happen."

She chuckled softly, cupping her stomach with her free hand. "The hell do you expect me to be able to do, chained up in here?" Her voice lowered when she added, "Call Asylum. He will be able to fix this."

"No, they will know that I…"

"Look." Femi inhaled a deep breath, wincing momentarily. "I don't care if you have to go to another city outside of Lima and pay a stranger to let you use their phone so it can't be traced to you. Asylum is my only way out of this. Now man the fuck up and show me that my father didn't waste his time and effort training you."

She stared into his eyes, hoping like hell he'd change his mind.

"Okay. Recite the number; I can't make it obvious that I'm putting it in my phone…"

Femi

She'd been back in Peru, according to Tatum, for three days. For that entire length of time, Femi hadn't been able to sleep, eat, or shower. No one took her to the bathroom, so she had to relieve herself in her pants. Her stomach, though empty, was severely bloated before she refused to do anything but pee on herself. Femi was at her lowest, weakest point in life... but as she stood in the center of The Bosses, you wouldn't have known that.

If she was going to die, it was going to be like a G – with strength. And honor. Dignity.

Looking every one of them in the eyes, Femi inhaled steady breaths. Her ribs were still a little sore, but they weren't broken, thankfully.

"Was it worth it?" Gabriel, the main boss, asked.

She thought over the fact that Anthony had still been alive, and she wanted to say no, but she wouldn't give them the satisfaction.

"You don't hear him speaking to you?" Nicholas, another boss, checked.

Keeping her eyes on Gabriel, Femi replied with, "I will reply when he says something worth replying to."

With one bob of his head, Nicholas instructed one of his men to slap Femi so hard, she immediately tasted blood.

"You were brought back to Peru to face punishment for going against The Bosses and taking revenge into your own hands," Gabriel informed, as if she didn't already know. "What do you think your punishment should be?"

"It doesn't matter what I think, you're going to kill me either way."

The room filled with silence. A smile slowly crept across Gabriel's face.

"You are your father's daughter." His smile fell.

If she weren't standing before him in handcuffs, she would have told him not to mention her father. Instead, she remained silent.

The sound of tires rolling and brakes screeching filled the open windows. Dust began to rise, gaining everyone's attention. No voices were heard, only the slamming of car door after car door. At the sound of a woman screaming, AK47's began to permeate their surroundings. Femi fell to her knees immediately as tears poured from her eyes. She didn't have to hear his voice to know he was there.

Asylum had come for her.

Two guards lifted her to her feet and drug her back to her cage. On her knees, she rocked back and forth as several different guns began to blast. The Bosses wouldn't lay down for anyone. They would not be taken out quietly. Though they were all over sixty and some of them were in wheelchairs and on oxygen machines, there were several men willing to risk their lives to save theirs.

Femi couldn't remember the last time she'd prayed, probably when her father was shot and she cried out to God for him to be spared, but she prayed now. Prayed as she continued to rock back and forth on her knees. Prayed that Asylum would make it out of this alive... even if she couldn't.

She wasn't sure how long they'd been at war, but eventually, the shooting and screaming, and cursing, and crying stopped. And so did her heart momentarily. Femi felt as if she held her breath the entire time she heard footsteps coming to her cage. When it finally opened and Asylum stepped inside with Rule and Tatum standing behind him... all she could do was cry.

20

Asylum

Though his feelings for Femi were permanent, Asylum knew their time together was temporary. That didn't make it easier to say goodbye, though. A month had passed since Asylum had rescued her, and so much in Peru had changed. Specifically Lima, Peru, where The Bosses operated out of. Without The Bosses, the city had gone mad. There was no order. No honor. No structure.

They needed a new leader.

They needed Femi.

After personally being called by the President of Peru, Femi knew she had to go back and restore order. Since she was responsible for the dismantling of The Bosses, it was her responsibility to rebuild. The old way of doing things had come to an end, and while a lot of people were happy about that... the president knew he'd need someone with power to restore the drug world or his city would be destroyed. While there was nothing he could do to stop it altogether, Femi was his only hope to manage it.

And she would give it her all.

Resting her head on Asylum's chest, Femi inhaled a deep breath.

They spent the entire night making love. Every time she was about to cry, she'd quickly leave the room. As much as that hurt, it made Asylum feel good, too, because it meant them parting ways was just as hard for her as it was for him.

It seemed as if their plans of getting married and starting a family would never happen, or at least no time soon. There was no way in hell she'd want to have a baby with her new position as The Boss of Peru. It would require too much time and effort. And quite frankly, it wouldn't be the safest job, either. While most of the country was happy The Bosses and their traditions were gone, some of their loyal supporters weren't.

Femi had proven that she could hold her own, though, and she'd have a full time, ten-man security team with her at all times.

That may not have been the life of a mother... but it was definitely the life for Femi.

"If you don't get in this car and leave, I won't be able to let you," Asylum warned, wrapping his arms tighter around her.

Femi lifted her head, looking up at him with a smile.

"The offer still stands for you to come to Peru. I know your foundation is here, but if you ever decide to leave things to Bailey and Diego, you know I will always have space reserved for you in my business, heart, and life."

Asylum nodded but remained silent. He'd considered becoming her partner and following her to Peru but decided against it. Though there was nothing besides the business and his friends keeping him here, it didn't feel right going there. Not right now at least. Femi still had a lot of work to do... personally. Within herself. She still hadn't been able to answer his questions, and until she could, Asylum wouldn't be comfortable uprooting his life for her. No matter how much he loved her.

Because if Femi didn't truly know herself, who was to say she wouldn't change and reinvent herself? And if she did, would she still want him? Would he still want her?

Nah.

That wasn't something Asylum was willing to risk.

He'd rather keep the memories they had in Memphis until she was truly ready for more.

"I'll keep that in mind."

Asylum placed a kiss to the center of her forehead, then opened the door to her car. Once he made sure she was inside securely, Asylum turned away, unable to watch her drive out of his life. As her car began to reverse, he fought within himself. He wanted to stop her, tell her he loved her, force her to learn herself and be content with herself so she could be content with him. But he couldn't do that. Instead, he hung his head and waited until he no longer heard the sound of her car before heading back into his home to try and figure out how in the hell he was supposed to do life without her.

Epilogue

Asylum
Six months later

ASYLUM WATCHED as Femi walked up the cracked concrete stairs to get to her heavily guarded mansion. She was the most beautiful vision in white that he'd ever seen – protruding belly and all. She was far enough along in her pregnancy now to no longer be able to hide it.

As usual, her eyes were covered with dark sunglasses, her hair was pulled up into a bun, and black lipstick covered her plump lips. She'd spent the day meeting with the president, her workers, and her old crew... and she still managed to stride effortlessly in her six-inch heels.

When Femi first left, Asylum was committed to letting her go and allowing her to do her own thing. Unfortunately, she fucked around and let it slip out to Camryn that she was pregnant. And she told Rule. And Rule told Asylum. At first, Asylum was angry because he thought Femi was trying to keep that from him, but

Camryn assured him that she planned to tell him a couple of weeks before she went into labor.

That wasn't good enough for Asylum, though.

There was no way in hell he'd miss this moment for anything in the world. And Femi would be out her damn mind if she thought he was going to be in a completely different country from his child. It was hard enough keeping his distance from her, but he wasn't even going to try and keep his distance from their child. Not a baby that was made in so much love. Love that they both needed to survive.

It took a few minutes, but eventually, Femi made it into her home and back into his line of view. Her bedroom was on the second floor. Because of the open window, he had the perfect visual on her. He watched as she pulled the dress over her head, smiling even more at the sight of her belly… and the tattoo of his name in the center of her neck.

Pride swelled within his heart. Not just because she'd gotten his name tatted on her, but because she'd gotten it on her throat chakra – acknowledging that she was willing to accept and receive everything he had to offer to her.

He found out that she was pregnant four months ago, and ever since, Asylum had been making moves to leave all of his shares of the business to Bailey and Diego. As far as he was concerned, Memphis would be a distant memory and Peru would be his new home for as long as Femi wanted to stay there. She walked away from the window, and Asylum called her phone. He needed to see her again, and she had a habit of gazing out of the window when she was talking or in deep thought.

As Asylum expected her to, Femi returned to the window as she answered his call.

EPILOGUE | 115

"Who are you?" he asked, hoping this time she'd finally have an answer.

Smiling, Femi placed her hand on her stomach. "I am Femi – just Femi. I removed my father's last name because... I didn't want to be shaped by him or my mother's pain. My past. I am me. A woman. A vessel of spirituality trying to become more in tune with God. I'm emotion, and strength, and courage, and passion, and fear, and weakness, and sadness, and love, and light..." She paused and chuckled. "I'm a Titan. The Boss of all Bosses. A living legend called to bring order and wealth to a fallen people. I—I'm Femi. A spirit, a heart. In desperate need of love. And the courage to love. Freely."

"And what do you desire?"

She scratched her ear. Squeezed the back of her neck. Licked her lips. Rubbed her belly.

"Time. A year max more here. That should give me enough time to get a team in place who can do what needs to be done here. Then, I desire to retire from the game and move somewhere by a beach. Somewhere I can be normal and live a life of love. And peace. Somewhere we can safely start a family. Teach our babies what it's like to grow up in a house filled with love. Faith. No fear. I desire a new identity. New interests and passion. New purpose. But most of all... I desire you."

Asylum smiled as he stared at her through the window.

"Then you will have me, and I'm going to do everything in my power to make sure you have everything else you desire, too."

Her head hung as she smiled. "I miss you so much, Asylum."

"I miss you, too."

"I wish I could see you. Touch you. Hold you."

He chuckled quietly as he opened the door. "You will... soon."

The End!

Made in the USA
Columbia, SC
09 November 2022